Andy

Books by

Mary Christner Borntrager

Ellie

Rebecca

Rachel

Daniel

Reuben

Andy

Andy

Mary Christner Borntrager

HERALD PRESS
Scottdale, Pennsylvania
Waterloo, Ontario

Library of Congress Cataloging-in-Publication Data
Borntrager, Mary Christner, 1921-
Andy / Mary Christner Borntrager.
p. ; cm. — (Ellie's people ; 6)
Summary: An overweight, short-tempered Amish teenager learns to control his eating habits and his anger after running away to live as a hobo.
ISBN 0-8361-3633-0
1. Amish—United States—Fiction. [1. Amish—Fiction. 2. Overweight persons—Fiction. 3. Conduct of life—Fiction. 4. Runaways—Fiction.] I. Title. II. Series: Borntrager, Mary Christner, 1921- Ellie's people ; 6.
[PS3552.07544A84 1993]
813'.54—dc20
[Fic] 93-20059
CIP
AC

The paper used in this publication is recycled and meets the minimum requirements of American National Standard for Information Sciences—Permanence of Paper for Printed Library Materials. ANSI Z39.48-1984.

Library of Congress Catalog Card Number: 93-20059
International Standard Book Number: 0-8361-3633-0
Printed in the United States of America
Cover art by Edwin Wallace/Book design by Paula M. Johnson

02 01 00 99 98 97 96 95 94 93 12 11 10 9 8 7 6 5 4 3 2

33,000 copies of this book in print in all editions

To my many friends
who have encouraged me
to keep writing

Contents

1
The Drifter

Andy saw him coming down the dusty road. He just knew the man would stop at their house.

"Look, Mom!" Andy exclaimed, leaning on his hoe handle. *"Er kummt* (he comes)!"

"Wer kummt (who comes)?" asked Lizzie.

"Why, *en Landleefer* (a tramp). See, he's just now crossing the bridge."

Lizzie squinted her eyes and peered through the sun's bright rays. She had married a fine young Amish boy, Jacob Maust. As the years passed, their family had grown to number seven children. There were three boys and four girls, including one set of twin girls.

Andy was the youngest son. He and his mother were in the garden hoeing the corn. It was midafternoon, and they had been working together for about two hours.

Lizzie straightened her back and sighed. She wiped sweat from her face with her apron. *"Ya* (yes), I see him now. I hope he doesn't stop here, unless it's just for a bite to eat. I won't send anyone away hungry."

Andy knew she wouldn't. She had a kind heart and always had plenty of food handy.

"*Ach* (oh), how I wish your dad were here. These drifters always seem to come when he is not around."

"Are you afraid of him, Mom?" Andy asked.

"No, I'm not afraid. I know God will protect us. It's just that they often ask for work, and I don't know what to say."

"Would Dad give him work, do you think?"

"I'm almost sure he would. He usually does," Lizzie replied.

"Well then, why don't we?"

"Oh, no, I don't make those decisions, Andy. I leave that up to your dad. He knows best. Anyhow, we'd better get on with our hoeing."

Sure enough, the wayfaring man came close to the garden fence. He stopped and called out, "You there, could you spare a meal for a tired, hungry man?"

Lizzie looked up from her work. She did not like the looks of this man. He had a long, dark mustache and beady, steel-gray eyes. His hat was pulled down just above the eyebrows. A large dirty cloth pack was slung over one shoulder.

"Well," responded Lizzie, "I've never yet refused food to a hungry soul. Come up to the porch and wait there, or if you like, you can sit under that maple tree. It's sure warm today."

"That it is, that it is," the man agreed. "Hotter'n blazes!"

Lizzie didn't care for that kind of talk. She hurried

inside and noticed how cool it felt in the house. The windows were open, and huge trees shaded it from the scorching sun.

The twins were busy. Annie was making homemade noodles in the summer kitchen. Fannie was ironing dresses with one flatiron as another was heating on the cookstove.

"Who is *der Fremder* (the stranger) out in the yard?" Annie wondered.

"Ach, some drifter who wants something to eat," said her mother.

"Where did he come from?" Fannie wondered as she peered out.

"I don't know. I didn't ask him," Lizzie replied as she hustled to heat up some leftovers.

"Maybe I'll ask him what he has in that pack he carries on his back," Andy murmured from the window as he watched the stranger resting under a maple tree in the yard.

"You'll do no such thing!" Lizzie stated flatly. "It's none of our business, and maybe we're better off if we don't know."

"Maybe he'll want to show us," Andy mused hopefully.

"If he would want to, he'll just have to do it without us asking," Annie said, trying to appear wise.

"Here, Andy," called Lizzie, "help me carry his lunch out for him. And mind you don't ask about that big bundle."

"You are too much of a *gwunnerich Naas* (wonder nose)," Fannie told him, looking up from her ironing.

"I am not," Andy declared, picking up a tin cup and

pitcher of iced tea. He held the screen door for his mother, then let it close with a bang as he followed her onto the back porch.

"Why don't you come up to the porch?" Lizzie invited the stranger. "Here are some chairs and a bench to set your tray on. You may be more comfortable here."

"Thankie, ma'am," said the stranger. "Times are hard, and I'm not used to comforts. Thankie."

Andy wanted to stay and talk to this man, but Mother had said not to bother him.

Ten minutes later there was a loud rap at the door. Andy answered.

"Mom," he called, "he wants more."

"What are you talking about?" Lizzie asked. She was reaching for a mixing bowl and starting to get things ready for the family supper.

"The tramp," said Andy. "The tramp wants to know if he can have more to eat."

"Don't you call me that, boy!" scolded the stranger, opening the screen door and taking hold of Andy's suspenders.

Although Andy was only thirteen, he was stoutly built and quite nervy, especially in front of his sisters.

"Well, you never told us your name," Andy countered, his eyes challenging this ruffian.

"Call me Cloyce. Cloyce Rader."

"Okay, Cloyce, relax! My mom will fix you another plate."

"That's more like it," Cloyce declared, returning to his seat on the porch.

"Umvergleichlich (weird)! How much can he eat?" exclaimed Annie.

"Well, I don't know," puzzled Lizzie, "but I hope he leaves after this plateful."

However, the stranger didn't leave. He made himself comfortable in the shade of a tree, waiting for Andy's dad to come in from the field.

2
Smokehouse Home

Andy was a robust boy, too heavy for his age and height. Because of this, other children teased him without mercy. He suffered as the target of many unkind remarks.

Food was a comfort to Andy, and he often consoled himself with it. Somehow it became a vicious cycle. He ate because he was unhappy. He was unhappy because he was too heavy.

Andy also had a problem with his temper. He was spoiled by his five older siblings, and his younger sister, Esther, usually looked up to him.

Even his father was more lenient with this youngest son. When Andy was three or four, his dad thought it seemed cute to see him display *Schpank* (spunk), as he called it.

His mother, however, had other thoughts. She was concerned for Andy's spiritual well-being and growth as well as his physical condition.

"Mom," asked Andy, "do you think he can stay?"

"Can who stay?"

"Why, Cloyce, the tramp."

"Andy," his mother cautioned, "I don't want you calling him a tramp. He was quite upset with you earlier when you used that word."

"*Er schrecke mich net* (he doesn't scare me)! If he tries to make trouble, I'll just sic Shep on him. That'll make him back off," Andy bragged.

"What makes you think one pup could handle a big man like that?" bantered his sister Annie.

" 'Cause," Andy answered, "he's not as big as a cow, and the cows pay attention to Shep."

"Well, this fellow doesn't look like a cow to me!" Annie laughed and rolled her eyes.

Andy stood at the window and watched the drifter lying under the maple tree, using his pack for a pillow. "I want him to stay. I want to know where he came from and where he's going and what he has in that big pack he carries."

"It's for your father to decide whether he stays or not. Really, I hope he doesn't," Lizzie said. "But regardless, Andy, we must not pry into his business. He didn't ask about work, so maybe he only wants to rest awhile."

"Oh," Andy reported, "when I brought in his empty plate the last time, he asked, 'Where's your old man?' I told him that he's in the *Feld* (field) raking hay. He said he'd wait for him.

"Mom, why did he call Dad 'old man'? That's a funny way to talk."

"No funnier than saying *Feld* for field. That's just his

way of talking. Bring in some more wood, Andy. Be sure to put the kindling on top as you stack it in the box. I'm baking corn pone for supper, and I need to have a good fire going."

Andy loved corn pone. Andy loved *all* food. With gusto he piled the woodbox full.

As he ran to the outside pump for a cool drink of water, he saw his father coming from the field, riding on the rake pulled by a team of horses.

Just then Andy's older brother Sammie was herding the cows into the barnyard to be handy for the evening milking. Their faithful collie, Shep, kept them in line by nipping at the heels of any who strayed.

Sammie had been hoeing burdock out of the pasture. Burdock and thistles seemed like everlasting enemies to him. He was glad it was time to quit.

"He's here!" shouted Andy, as he ran huffing and puffing to meet his dad and brother.

"Who's here? Who are you talking about?" asked Sammie.

"The tramp, I mean, the drifter under our tree," Andy panted, all out of breath.

"You make about as much sense as these cows," Sammie complained. "And stop your yelling! You'll scare them so they won't let their milk down right."

"Well, you wait till you see him. *Er guckt wie er is verhafdich ebbes* (he looks like he's really something)! Someone important!" Andy exclaimed as he ran off to catch up with his dad.

Jake Maust stopped his horses. "*Well, nau, was gibt's* (well, now, what's the matter)?" he asked his son.

"A man came to the house this afternoon and asked

for something to eat. Mom gave him two big plates of food, and now he's resting under the maple tree. Mom thinks he wants to ask you for work. She says she doesn't care for him to stay—but I do.

"He looks so interesting. You know what? He has a black mustache, and all he carried is a cloth bag. Dad, I wonder what he has in there. Are you going to let him stay? Will you give him work, huh?"

"If you quit talking long enough, Andy, I might think about it."

"Oh, good, good!"

"*Waard mol* (wait once)," said his father, "I haven't even seen this man yet, and of course your mother and I need to talk about it."

Jake drove up to the barn and unhitched his team. As he opened the barn door, he heard someone behind him say, "Howdy." It was the stranger who had stopped for a bite to eat.

"My name is Cloyce Rader. Your good wife gave me some food to eat today, and I'd be much obliged if I could work for you a spell. I'm strong and not afraid of hard work."

"Well," responded Jake, "my wife and I always decide such things together. Tell you what—we'll talk about it over supper."

After a lengthy discussion, Jake and Lizzie decided that the stranger could stay on a trial basis.

"But where will we put him, Jake?" Lizzie asked her husband. "Our beds are all full, and when Ellie and Roy come home on weekends, we have to set up cots for them."

Their oldest children were working on nearby

farms, Ellie as a *Maut* (hired girl) and Roy as a *glee Gnecht* (hired boy).

"I think we'll fix up the smokehouse for him," suggested Jake. "It's small, but it does have a window. Big enough for one man.

"Tonight he can sleep in the barn. Then tomorrow Andy and the girls can fix up a place for him. Put a folding cot out there, and the old dresser from the attic. He can set the washbasin on an apple crate. That chair on the back porch isn't used much anymore, so take that."

"I'll let them take that old lampstand from the *Keller* (basement)," offered Lizzie, "and a Bible. We need to make sure he has a Bible."

"Ya," agreed Jake, "*das is gut* (that's good)."

Thus it happened that the smokehouse became a little home. Andy helped arrange things there. Then he showed everything to Cloyce, who seemed to be satisfied.

Andy was excited to have a stranger living on the farm.

3
Faraway Places

Andy heard it. He was sure he did. It came from the direction of the smokehouse.

Jake had told his son to stay away from there and not bother Cloyce after working hours. It had been three weeks since this man came, and not once had Andy disobeyed that rule. But now he could not resist.

Such beautiful music he never heard before. In fact, Andy seldom heard any music other than the sounds of nature or of singing. Musical instruments were *verbodde* (forbidden) in Amish homes.

Now Andy thought he just must see what Cloyce was up to.

Creeping to the shanty, he hoisted himself up on a piece of firewood to look in the window. There sat Cloyce playing and singing.

Andy had never seen such an instrument before. It looked like a long-handled wooden paddle with strings. Cloyce made music come from that with his fingers. He was singing something about "land, lots of land," and "don't fence me in."

The piece of a log Andy had been standing on shifted, and he lost his footing. Down he went with a crash.

The noise brought Cloyce to his feet immediately, and the door opened. Even though Andy tried to run, he was stopped in his tracks as a rough hand grabbed his shirt by the back of the neck.

"What are you doing out here, boy?" Cloyce asked.

Andy was shaking so badly that he couldn't answer.

"Come on, boy. I asked you a question."

"I was listening to you sing and to the music," Andy whimpered.

The hand that gripped Andy's shirt loosened a bit. "So, you like my singing and playing, do you? Well, come on inside, and I'll show you some real pickin'."

"But I'm not supposed to bother you."

"Who says it's a bother?"

"My mom and dad, they told me."

"If I invite you, then that's different. Don't you agree?"

"Well, maybe. But first I'd better go and ask."

"What's your name? I can't remember, but it won't do to keep calling you 'boy.' "

"My name's Andy."

"It gets mighty lonesome here at night sometimes, Andy, so I'd be pleasured if you sit a spell with me. Anyway, I want to ask you some questions.

"I like your spunk, Andy. You get teased a lot by other kids, don't you? When your folks had company, I heard them calling you 'Fatty, Fatty, two-by-four,' and 'Andy, Andy, want some candy?'

"Don't blame you for gettin' riled. Don't blame you a'tall. Now, are you comin' in or aren't you?"

Andy was still amazed at the sudden change in the attitude of Cloyce.

"Come on. I'll tell your old man I asked you to come in my house." Cloyce let out a guffaw as Andy gingerly stepped through the open doorway. "Here, sit on the cot. I like to sit on the chair to do my performance." He snorted out another laugh.

First he played "Tumblin' Tumbleweed." Then upon a request from Andy, he again played and sang "Don't Fence Me In."

"Why do you people dress and talk different?" Cloyce asked.

"Because we're Amish," Andy replied.

"What's Amish?"

"It's when you can't have any worldly things."

"Like what?"

"Ach, like cars, or telephones and electricity, or tractors."

"Why do your ma and sisters wear such plain, long dresses and those funny-looking caps?"

"They're Amish and are supposed to." Andy simply answered the best he knew how.

"I sure wouldn't want to live that way if I wouldn't have to. Say, you work pretty hard for a boy your age. What do you do for fun?"

"I like best to go down to the creek—just me and our dog—and I like to play with our baby animals. When I'm alone, no one teases me."

"I like to be alone, too," Cloyce told Andy. "Don't do for me to stay put in one place long. I'm a rambler. Yes sir, you should hear about all the wonderful sights I've seen.

"I've been way out West where the sky is so blue and the water so clear you can see right to the bottom. Ain't many trees, though, just miles and miles of prairie.

"I remember the beautiful, golden grain in the Kansas wheat fields, and the green cornfields of Iowa. It's a sight, boy. It purely is. Some of the big towns I've been to—why, Andy, the buildings look like they reach to the clouds."

"No!" exclaimed Andy.

"Yes, they do. That's why they're called skyscrapers. I've rode me many a freight train and seen some faraway places. In California, trees grow so big you can drive a car right through the trunk."

A loud knock sounded on the smokehouse door. Cloyce answered, and there stood Jake Maust.

"Is my son in here?" he asked.

"Yes, he is, mister," said Cloyce.

"Andy, go to the barn and wait for me," Jake sternly commanded him.

"Wait a minute," Cloyce said. "I asked him to come in."

"He's been told to stay away from the smokehouse and not bother you," Jake stated.

"No bother, none at all."

"That's not the point. I'm his father, and he's to obey."

Jake turned and walked toward the barn. He had a talk with his son and then punished him for disobeying. Andy knew he deserved what he got.

"From now on," said Father, "Cloyce may tell us of his travels while we rest on the porch or under the shade trees. As for playing music, that's not for our people. I'm telling you once more, stay away from the smokehouse."

Andy went to bed with a sorry heart because he had done wrong. But he could not forget those faraway places. Someday he would see them for himself. Someday, when he was all grown up.

4
He's Gone!

Friday night couldn't come too soon for Andy Maust. School would be all right if his classmates were kinder, he thought.

Andy loved books. Many times he pretended to be the hero in a story. This brought him almost as much comfort as spending time with his animals or eating.

"Andy," called Lizzie as he got home from school, "*kumm mol do* (come here once)."

"*Was wit* (what do you want)?" he asked.

"Dad wants you to take the cows and pasture them along the roadside for an hour or so. The grass in our field is getting short."

"Oh, good!" Andy exclaimed. He loved the outdoors, and he loved animals.

"*Waard* (wait)!" Lizzie called to him. "You must take Shep along. He's a good cattle dog. They'll stay in line for him. I'll send Esther out to let you know when to bring the cows in."

"Ya, Mom. *Ich geb achtsam* (I'll be careful)."

After he changed to his work clothes, Andy ran outside and called the family dog. On his way, he grabbed several just-baked cookies.

"Here, Shep," he called. Around the corner of the house came the dog, wagging his tail with excitement.

"Ya, Shep, *du bist froh mich zehne* (you're glad to see me)," Andy said. He gave the dog a piece of cookie. "I wish the kids at school, and at church, too, would be happy to see me like you are, Shep." Andy reached down and patted the collie.

"Come on, boy, we have to bring the cows in." He opened the barnyard gate and started for the field. Most of the cows stood listlessly chewing their cud or lying under some shade trees.

The instant Andy said, "Go get 'em, boy," Shep knew what he was to do. He headed in the direction of the cows. Barking and nipping at their tails or heels, he soon had them moving in a straight line toward the barnyard.

"That Shep, now he's a smart dog. I guess Johnny, Levi, Enos, and none of the other boys have one so smart," Andy mused to himself.

"Cloyce likes you, too." This time the remark was directed to Shep, who wagged his tail all the harder.

His younger sister, Esther, was waiting by the lane to help Andy get the cows started in the right direction. It didn't take long because the tall green grass looked inviting to the hungry cows.

"Esther," called Andy as soon as the cows began to eat. "Esther, bring me some cookies, a few crackers, and a jar of water."

"Ach, my!" Esther exclaimed. "If you don't quit eating so much, you'll get as big as these critters." She pointed to the cattle who were already cropping the grass.

"I will not!" fumed Andy. "You bring me some or I'll come get them myself."

"And leave the cows alone? Ei-yi-yi!"

"Well then, you bring me some," Andy demanded. His neck and face turned red, as they often did if he was angry.

"*Mir gucke mol* (we'll see once)." His sister turned to the house.

Later she came back with one cookie and a few crackers, plus a jar of water. "Mom said this is all you can have before supper."

Andy quickly reached for the morsels she brought and wished for an early evening meal.

He loved to watch the cows wrap their tongues around the clumps of orchard grass. He listened to the chomp, chomp as they bit the grass and the squeak, squeak as they tore off each mouthful because they had teeth only on the bottom jaw.

Lying on his back, he watched soft white clouds drifting by. He thought once more of those faraway places Cloyce told him about. He vowed to see them for himself someday.

Just then a big blue fly buzzed close to his ear. It startled him, and he forgot to watch the cows. They were almost at the end of the road. Shep was waiting there to turn them back toward Andy.

"I hope Shep minds his business," Andy told himself out loud. The dog did his duty, and soon it was time to take the cows in for the evening milking. Esther again helped herd them back into the farmyard for chore time.

Father and Cloyce had just come from the field. They were hot and thirsty. Cloyce was glad the weekend was approaching. He was not afraid of hard work, but Sundays he slept much of the day or played his guitar. As a boy he had been taught the Scriptures, he had told them, but now he was not a churchgoing man.

"I hope Cloyce reads that Bible we put in his shack," Lizzie remarked. "God can do what we can't. He can change a hard heart."

"Ya, *sell is so* (that is so)," agreed Jake.

Andy did not think Cloyce had a hard heart at all. The new farmhand had told him a lot of interesting things.

Last week though, Cloyce dropped a paper from his hip pocket, and when Andy picked it up, he snatched it away quickly. "You give that here!" he demanded, his eyes narrowing to mere slits. "Don't you ever tell anyone you saw this. Understand?"

For the first time, Andy was afraid of this man. He hadn't really seen anything except some numbers and a picture that looked like Cloyce.

"Promise me, upon your word of honor, you won't mention this even to your old man."

Andy didn't know what "word of honor" meant, but he promised.

"Okay, Andy," Cloyce ordered, "forget this even happened."

Sunday was a rainy day. Cloyce did not come to the house for breakfast.

"Ach, *loss ihn schlofe* (let him sleep)," said Jake. "He will be hungry enough by the time we get home from church at the Eash's place."

By two in the afternoon there was still no sign of the drifter. "Andy, go and knock on the door of the smokehouse. See if Cloyce wants anything to eat. He's a hard worker and must be hungry."

Andy hurried to the shanty, but in a few minutes he came running back. "He's gone, Dad, he's gone!"

"Who's gone, Andy?" Jake asked.

"Cloyce! Cloyce is gone, and the door of the smokehouse was wide open. It rained in there, and some things are wet."

"Ach, *mei Hatz* (my heart)!" exclaimed Lizzie.

"He really is gone!" Andy announced once more.

5
Fish Rock Creek

It was a good place to be alone. Right now that's what Andy wanted. Fish Rock Creek cut through Jake Maust's farm just above the orchard. It meandered its way through the pasture and along the woods. A half mile downstream, it made a sharp bend onto the Swartz farm.

The young Amish boys claimed a deep spot at the bend as their swimming hole. Andy sometimes joined them, but often he was ridiculed. However, if the Wagler boys were among the group, it was different. Their parents taught them to be friends with everyone, especially those who were mistreated.

After Andy discovered that Cloyce had left, Lizzie sent the twins to help Andy get the wet bedding out of the smokehouse. That done, Andy just wanted to get away so he could think. There was still half of a Sunday afternoon of free time ahead, so he asked his dad for permission to go to the creek.

"*Was wit do* (what do you want there)?" his father wondered.

"Maybe I can see that big fish the Swartz boys have been trying to catch," Andy replied.

"Ach, those boys talk pretty tall. Do you really believe there is such a big fish there?"

"The Wagler boys said they saw him. If he's in there, Dad, I'd like to see him. Just once, so I can tell how long he really is."

"What would you do if you did see him? Catch him with your *blutte Hend* (bare hands)?" Sammie laughed as he pretended to be grabbing a fish.

"*Du bist dumm* (you're dumb)," Andy told his brother. "I know better than that. All you can think about is that girl." He kicked against the screen door, putting a small hole in the screen.

Sammie had been taking a girl home from Sunday evening youth singings. Since he had been casting glances at Rhoda Mullet for some time, the family was fairly sure she was the one.

"Now *guck* (look) what you did, Andy. That little hole in the screen will get bigger and bigger. Why do you always let things make you so angry?" Lizzie asked.

"Maybe you should stay home and patch the screen," Jake told his son.

"Dad," Sammie offered, "I'll fix it. I shouldn't have teased him."

"Well, if you feel that way, Sammie, I guess it's all right. But Andy, you can only stay at the creek for an hour. I had thought I'd let you go for the rest of the afternoon, but until you learn to control that temper, we must use some restrictions. Sammie was just having some fun with you."

"Some fun!" muttered Andy.

"Dad," Sammie said, "could my family start calling me Sam instead of Sammie? I'm a man now, and it doesn't sound right anymore."

"Zu gross fer dei Hosse (too big for your britches)," laughed Jake. "Well, we can try, but it will take some doing. Sammie it's always been."

"I guess it wouldn't do to call your wife the Sammie Rhoda," quipped his mother. "Sam Rhoda sounds better."

Sam grinned and rolled his eyes. He knew that his people identified each other this way because of so many similar names. But he wasn't going to admit anything about Rhoda!

Andy thought it silly to change his brother's name now. He dashed out of the house, called Shep, and headed for the creek.

First Cloyce left, and now Sammie was changing his name. Before long Ellie and Roy might be getting married. Things would never be the same.

Andy gathered half a dozen flat stones and skipped them across the water. He loved skipping stones. The most he had ever done was seven skips. Danny Wagler had a record of ten. Of course, the Swartz boys boasted twelve, but no one had seen them do it.

Shep was running here and there, chasing chattering squirrels. Once in a while he startled a rabbit and ran in hot pursuit.

Suddenly Shep stopped and sniffed a spot on the ground. He whined softly.

"What is it, Shep?" Andy came to investigate. "Why, that looks like the pocket watch that Dad said he lost. But Dad hasn't been down here for a long time."

Shep ran a little further, pulled a piece of paper out of the sand, and brought it to Andy.

"Ach, Shep, you drag anything around. It's just a piece of paper. Here, let me have it, and I'll make a paper boat to sail," Andy said as he reached toward Shep.

"Dut dei Hund schwetze (does your dog talk)?" someone asked.

Andy looked up the creek bank into the smirking faces of Johnny and Joey Swartz. He knew they would tease him. His anger began to show as he said, *"Geht heem* (go home)!"

"Are you going to make us go?" Joey asked.

"Maybe I will. This is our property," Andy reminded them.

"Fish Rock belongs to everybody," Johnny claimed as he picked up a stone to skip on the water.

"What's that paper you're holding?" Joey asked, trying to snatch it.

Shep came to Andy's aid and took the paper between his teeth. The dog ran toward the bend in the creek. Andy called him back, but Johnny threw his stone after Shep for all he was worth.

Poor Shep fell to the ground and howled in pain. The dropped paper fluttered away in the breeze.

Andy took off after the boys. When they saw the damage they had caused, they ran for home as fast as they could.

"Oh, Shep," Andy cried as he knelt by his beloved dog. "Oh, Shep, will you be alright?"

Slowly the dog rose to his feet, and Andy gave him a big hug.

"Let's go home, Shep," Andy said, patting the beautiful head of the collie. He started walking with his beloved Shep limping alongside.

"I wish those boys weren't so mean. I'm glad, though, I still have the watch we found.

"That paper—it's lost. Shep, it sure looked a lot like the paper that drifter made me promise to keep secret. Do you suppose Cloyce was here by the creek after he left? I wonder."

6
The Agreement

Jake was glad to get his watch back. "Where did you find it, Andy?" he asked.

"Down by the creek, Dad. Shep saw it first. He found something else, too, but the Swartz boys made him drop it. Johnny threw a stone at him and knocked him down. He hit Shep on his leg," Andy stormed.

"I know it hurt because Shep limped all the way home. I wish I had hit Johnny with a stone. Then I'd see how he liked it." Andy swung his throwing arm.

"*Wie oft miss ich dir saage* (how often must I tell you), Andy? Returning evil for evil never solves anything. Have you tried to be nice to them?"

"I can't be nice to boys like that. They just call me *Fettkessel* (lard kettle) and *Maus* (mouse). They say our name Maust means we're like mice."

"Let them say on. We are what we make ourselves by our deeds and actions. I just hope you don't call them names."

Andy didn't admit that he had done that very thing more than once. He especially liked to call the Swartz boys *Schwatzbaert* (blackbeards, pirates).

"But, Dad, they hurt Shep, and he can't protect himself."

"Ach, I suspect he can. Come on, I'll take a look at that leg."

Andy followed his father out to the edge of the walk where Shep lay. The dog wanted to come up on the porch, but he knew that was off limits for him.

Many times Lizzie or one of the girls had chased him off the porch with the broom. They never hit Shep, just shooed him away.

"He tracks too much mud," Lizzie told Andy.

"But, Mom, he likes to be where it's warm," her son protested.

"The barn, buggy shed, workshop, and toolshed are warmer than the open porch. Shep can go there for shelter."

Jake examined Shep's leg. He saw how the dog favored the right front one.

"There's a small knot here." Jake pointed to a spot the size of a quarter. "It's just a bruise and should heal quickly."

"Just a bruise!" Andy shouted, his face turning beet red. "If I catch those Swartz boys, I'll give *them* a bruise!"

"*Genunk* (enough)!" Jake declared.

"Andy, you remember you asked me a few weeks ago if you could build a doghouse for Shep? Well, I'll make an agreement with you. If you'll try to control that temper, I'll give you permission to build one.

"You can't control it by yourself. I know of One who can help you. Do you know who I mean?"

"Yes, Dad. But how can I do it? Don't you mind when people make *Schpott* (fun) of us?"

"I don't like it, Andy, but they are doing more harm to themselves than to me. It makes me feel sorry for them.

"I'm sure Lester Swartz and his wife don't want their sons to act so rudely. Maybe I should talk to Lester about their behavior."

"No, I don't want you to do that," Andy quickly remarked.

"Fer was net (why not)?"

"If you do, they'll tease me more. One time I said I would tell on them for stealing. They called me a *Grossmaulbuppli* (big-mouth baby)."

"So you didn't tell? Did that make them like you any better? Were you helping them get away with stealing by keeping it a secret?"

These were hard questions for Andy. Was Dad ever thirteen years old? he wondered. Dad just doesn't understand how hard it is for me to be teased all the time.

So he changed the subject. "How long before I can build Shep's house?"

"That depends. Let's see how well you can behave."

"I wish Sammie could help me build it. But all he wants to do is think about going to singings with his girl."

"Try calling him Sam instead of Sammie, and maybe he'll help you," suggested Jake.

"He's been Sammie for so long, I forget that he

wants his name changed now."

"So do I. But as soon as I remember, I say Sam. Andy, it looks like it might rain again. Why don't you take Shep and fix him a bed in the barn for the night. Sam's fetching the cows so we can milk right after supper."

Andy picked up Shep and carried him to the barn, all thirty pounds of him. The dog could have walked, but Andy's heart ached for him. He knew too well how it felt to be mistreated.

"Here, Shep, I'll fix you a nice warm place under Star's feedbox. You like horses, and they like you, especially Star does.

"I'll bring you some water, too, after supper. If Mom lets me, I'll get some table scraps for you later. I know you'd like that."

He arranged soft clean straw under the manger and petted Shep's sides and head gently.

True to his promise, after supper Andy carried a pan of clean water and leftover meat scraps to his faithful companion. Then after milking, he secured the door tightly against the threatening storm and went to the house and to bed.

At first sleep would not come. He thought of the events of his day. He had gone to Fish Rock Creek to catch sight of a big fish. Not one glimpse of him did he see.

He wondered again how his dad's pocket watch came to be there. Then there was that mysterious paper Shep had found. If it weren't for those Swartz boys, he might know what it was about.

Johnny was so cruel to Shep! And as always, his

temper flared up again. If only he could handle that better!

Andy remembered again the agreement with his Dad about building a doghouse. He knew just how he wanted it built. Andy whispered a prayer, "God, help me keep my temper so Dad will let me make that doghouse."

The storm broke, and Andy heard rain rattling his window. He was glad Shep was safe and warm in the barn.

Everything seemed all right again, and finally Andy slept.

7
An Extra Hand

Fall was a beautiful time as usual, with the leaves turning glorious colors of red, orange, and yellow. It was also a busy time.

Andy and Esther were back in school, but each afternoon they had extra chores to do because Jake and Sam were busy in the fields.

"We must get our winter wheat sowed and our corn cut and husked," Jake told his family one Saturday at breakfast. "The Lord has given us such a good harvest. I'll need to build another crib for the corn. And before winter is over, we'll need more farrowing pens for the sows and piglets.

"Sam, I hope you don't get married too soon. There is a lot to do around here," Jake joked, pretending to look serious.

"Come on, Dad," Sam answered, "I'm not getting married this fall. Even if I were, you know we'll be just as busy five years from now as we are today.

"Anyhow, all these girls should have been boys," he said, looking at his sisters seated at the table.

They groaned in mock despair.

"If all girls were boys, then who would you take home from singings?" asked Annie.

"Oh, well, you could work harder on Monday if you didn't stay out so late on Sunday nights," commented Fannie.

"If I finally found someone to have me, you wouldn't spoil it, would you?" Sam cast soulful eyes at his sisters. This brought laughter and more jolly remarks.

"Fannie and Annie can do some of the husking," Mother offered, "but I'll also need them to help put away the rest of the garden things for the winter. We have a lot of canning to do."

"You can just say no when people come asking for a *Maut* (hired girl). If you need more help, keep Ellie home for yourself," advised her husband.

"Well, she's old enough to work out, and other families with only young children need her," Lizzie reminded Jake. "And the same thing goes for Roy, too. At their age, it's good for them to get around and learn to know other families."

Esther was too frail to help with much outside work. She had struggled through an attack of rheumatic fever when quite young, and she was not yet as robust as the other children. Yet she could handle many light jobs around the house and garden.

"Well," decided Jake, "I may just need to hire an extra hand for a while until we catch up with some work around here."

An extra hand meant another man or boy. Now Andy was happy again.

"Dad," he asked, "will it be Cloyce? You said he was a good worker."

"He may have been a good worker, but he sure isn't dependable. We don't even know where he is."

"Let's ask around in town or at the Thursday auctions. Someone might have seen him," Andy suggested. "Maybe he's looking for a job again."

"No, Andy, I want an Amish boy, one who understands our ways. They know how we want things done."

"I'd work right along with Cloyce," offered Andy. "I'd teach him how we do things."

"Well, you'll be in school most days and won't be here to teach him. Anyhow, why do you want him back?" Jake asked.

"He didn't make *Schpott* (fun) of me. I liked when he told me of all the places where he'd been. You should have heard his stories, Dad. He sure saw some sights."

"Ach, he *was* a sight, if you ask me," Lizzie remarked. "That big scraggly mustache and those shifty eyes! I never did trust him. It wonders me now if he took your pocket watch, Jake, and lost it down by the Fish Rock."

Andy couldn't believe that Cloyce would steal. He didn't *want* to believe it. Cloyce seemed like a mysterious but fair guy to him.

"Mom," Andy ventured, "it sounds as if you don't like Cloyce, just because he isn't Amish."

"That has nothing to do with it," Lizzie defended herself. "I didn't say I don't like him. We are to love everyone, but we need not like what they do. He has a soul that's of as much worth to God as anyone's.

"He was hungry when he came here, and I fed him. But we need to be on guard against evil, to be wise as serpents and harmless as doves.

"Anyhow, you know he just disappeared without telling us he was going. So we really don't know who he is or where he is."

"Maybe he needed more than food," Andy remarked.

"Well, he's gone, and what's done is done," Jake said.

"We can't just sit around here all day talking. Grandpa Jesse told me Lester Swartz's oldest boy is eighteen and looking for work. I believe I'll take a run over there first thing this morning and see if he can help us for a while."

Andy wondered if he was hearing right. Surely his Dad wouldn't get one of those Swartz boys to help him. He knew how mean they could be. The oldest one—why, that would be Joey.

"Dad, are you really going to have Joey Swartz work for us? You know how he and Johnny treated Shep and me one afternoon. Couldn't you find someone else to help?"

"*Druwwle dich net* (don't trouble yourself). He may learn some things while he's here. Besides, those Swartz boys are good carpenters. I've watched them at barn raisings."

Andy saw that his dad's mind was made up. If Lester and Joey Swartz agreed, then Joey would be that extra hand for the Mausts.

Breakfast was over, and Jake gave Sam and Andy their work assignments before he left for the Swartz's place.

Andy sought solace in the company of Shep as he headed for the barn and his Saturday work of cleaning out hog pens.

He also comforted himself with a resolution: someday he would see the sights of the world as another extra hand had described them.

Yes, he would! Someday!

8
Torn Britches

"Since you're getting a hired man," Lizzie told Jake, "I'm glad it's Joey Swartz."

"Why so?" her husband asked.

"He lives close by, so that means he won't be boarding here. We will only need to give him his *Middaagesse* (noon meal)."

Andy secretly wished Joey wouldn't come at all. "Why, oh, why couldn't Roy come home and help us catch up with the work?" he muttered to himself.

One thing Andy was determined to do. He would keep as much space between Joey Swartz and himself as he could. This, however, would not be easy.

Monday morning came and with it came Joey. Shep barked at him, showing his disapproval as Joey rode his bicycle in the lane.

Undoubtedly Shep remembered when he had been hit down at Fish Rock Creek. The dog could not know it was Joey's brother who threw the stone at him. But by the way he yipped at Joey, he must have recognized that Joey was at the scene where it all happened.

"Andy, go out and call Shep down," Jake told his son.

Andy would rather have sicced the dog onto Joey, but he didn't. Instead he called Shep to his side, talked to him, and stroked the dog's fine head.

Joey heard the low guttural growl Shep made and slowly edged closer, but with a wary eye out for the dog.

"Du hast besser ihm hewe (you'd better hold him)," Joey warned. "If he bites me, you're in big trouble, Andy."

"I'm holding him, and he won't bite. He never did bite anyone. Go on in the house. Dad's in the kitchen."

Joey backed across the porch toward the screen door while watching the dog and then was glad to get inside away from Shep.

"Well, I see you're right on time. I like that," said Jake.

"I try never to be late," Joey stated. "Just one thing, though. Could you pen up that dog of yours while I'm here? I don't think he likes me."

Andy had come inside just as Joey made this request. He objected immediately. "Pen Shep up! No, Dad! He wouldn't like that. We've never penned him up."

To Andy's relief, his dad replied, "Ach, nah, that isn't necessary. He'll get used to you. Anyhow, why wouldn't he like you?"

This unexpected question caught Joey off guard. He stammered and struggled to answer. "Ach, well, my—ach, Johnny, he happened to . . . my younger brother somehow hit him with a stone one day by the creek. I didn't do it."

"Ya, *ich weese was gewwe hot* (I know what happened)," Jake said. "Now you must win Shep's confidence back. It may not be easy, but you can start by showing kindness to him and his master, too."

"His master?" Joey said, looking puzzled.

"*I'm* his master," Andy said. "He's my dog, isn't he, Dad?"

"He's the family dog, but he seems to claim you, Andy, and you claim him. In that case, you're his master.

"Well, we'd better get to work. Andy's staying home from school this week to help. Sam, you and Andy hitch the sorrels to the wagon and take some corn knives to open up the back cornfield. I'll help Joey get started building the new corncrib."

Andy was glad the older Amish boys had a week off from school for cornhusking. He did not like school. Most of the children teased him. He longed for the day he would be sixteen. Then he could quit.

However, books were a joy to him. Unlike some of his Amish cousins, he had access to many. Andy loved poetry and had written a few poems which earned him an excellent reward: a Barlow pocketknife from his teacher. Andy didn't know how handy that knife would be before this day ended.

During chore time Joey came to the barn to ask Jake Maust a question about measurements for the crib door. Shep was lying in the feedway, but when he saw Joey, he lost no time getting to his feet. Shep bared his teeth and growled, his hair bristling.

Joey also lost no time in making a run for the ladder to the hayloft. In his hurry, the seat of his pants caught on a large spike. There he hung yelling at the top of his voice, "*Kumm schnell! Er grickt mich* (come quick! he'll get me)!"

Andy wanted to laugh when he saw Joey's predicament. "*Er hot dich nau* (he has you now)."

"Make him go away, and help me down!" Joey begged.

"Maybe I will—sometime. But first you promise to be nice to him."

"I don't want anything to do with him. I won't bother him. Just make him go away."

"And do you promise not to be mean to me or make *Schpott* (fun)?" Andy asked. He was sure going to take advantage of this situation.

"I promise anything! Just cut me loose!"

"*Was geht's* (what gives)?" asked Jake, stepping into the feedway. He had heard the commotion and came to investigate.

"Joey is still afraid of Shep," Andy answered.

"Well, I'll show you how to be his friend. Andy, do you have your knife handy?"

It would have given Andy pleasure to leave Joey dangling for a while, but he obediently produced his trusty Barlow. Jake had Shep sniff the knife, and then he cut Joey free.

"Here now, Andy, you take your knife and give it to Joey."

"But it's my knife," protested Andy.

"I know, but give it to Joey so he can let Shep sniff it

again. It will have all our scents on it, and Shep should know it's all right."

Sure enough, the dog didn't growl at Joey this time.

"Pet him," Andy suggested to Joey.

Cautiously Joey patted Shep, and they started to tolerate each other.

Andy chuckled to himself all evening about how it took his Barlow knife and a pair of torn britches to bring Shep and Joey Swartz to an understanding.

"To get rid of an enemy, make him your friend," Jake told his son later.

9

No Doghouse Yet!

It was an exceptionally warm day for early November. Joey Swartz had only two more weeks to work for Jake Maust. He would be home by Thanksgiving Day.

The corncrib was built, and Jake had called a husking bee. Their people came from nearby farms one night to help them finish the corn. This frolic was a great social occasion and a chance for them to get together and help each other in time of need.

Jake calculated that they would have the farrowing pens completed within a week, and then they would check to make sure the barn was tight for the winter.

The harvest was over, so the family was looking forward to more relaxing days. Men were thinking of auctions and horse sales, while women dreamed of quilting bees and weddings.

"*Buwe* (boys)," said Jake, addressing Andy, Sam, and Joey at dinner one Saturday. "It's a nice day. You've worked hard all fall, so what say we take the afternoon off, and you can do what you like?"

This suited the boys fine. Sam wanted to get something for his rig from the carriage maker, so he left right away. Joey decided to go fishing, and Andy had other plans. They would be free for a few hours, they thought.

Their plans changed quickly, however. Esther came running and shouting, *"Daadi, die Kieh sin aus der Weed ausgebroche* (Dad, the cows have broken out of the pasture)!"

Sure enough! They were scattered all over, nipping grass and vegetables and flowers. Some had already run down the road and crossed the bridge. Worse yet, three were in Lizzie's large flower garden, and two were going down the rows of cabbage and taking a bite out of each head.

"Get Shep," Jake told Andy.

The faithful dog came bounding out of the barn at Andy's call. He soon sized up the situation. In no time at all, not one cow was in the flower bed or the garden. Lizzie came out to look over the damage, and she was not pleased!

Next Shep went to bring the strays in from the roadway. As usual, there was a stubborn one in the bunch. No matter how much Esther, Jake, the boys, and Shep narrowed the gap, Bossy the heifer escaped.

Andy's temper got the better of him again. He picked up a large stone and threw it hard at Bossy. The stone found its target. It struck the young heifer right behind her ear. She fell as if shot.

For a moment Bossy lay there. Jake quickly went to investigate the damage. Andy felt anger and fear at the same time. Then to his relief, Bossy rose to her feet and started toward the the farm lane with Shep at her heels.

"That Shep, now, he's some dog," Joey remarked.

"Ich weese (I know)," Andy agreed. He dreaded what his father would have to say about throwing that rock.

"Well, boys," Jake said after the cows were penned in the barnyard, "it looks like we'll have to change our plans for this afternoon. As soon as we find where these cattle broke out, there'll be fence to mend."

"These dumb cows," Andy fumed. "I was going to start work on Shep's doghouse. We have some short pieces of good leftover lumber. It would have been nice to work in the shop."

"No, Andy, you figured wrong," Jake said. "Don't you remember our agreement? I had told you, once you learn to control your temper, you may build a doghouse. What you did out there did not look like self-control to me."

"But Bossy made me so mad. Why couldn't she come in like the others did? Now you won't let me start on that house, and it's all her fault." Andy kicked a stick lying there in front of him.

"You're wrong, Andy. If you had not thrown that rock at Bossy, I would let you get started. I was even looking forward to helping you build it."

"You were?" Andy was surprised and started to think: *Why do I get angry so easily? It's not like me to hurt animals. Am I any better than Johnny, who hit Shep?*

How he wished he hadn't thrown that rock. But what was done was done. Andy could not undo the deed.

The boys followed Jake to the shop. "We'll get the things we need and see where those cows got out," Jake told them.

"Andy," he asked, after rummaging around among his tools, "have you seen my wire snips?"

"No," answered Andy.

"Well, that's strange. I bought a new pair last spring and only used them one day. I'm certain I put them on the hook right next to the level. Several things have come up missing since that Cloyce Rader left."

Andy didn't believe what his dad was saying. *Why does he always pick on Cloyce? Just because he's different, is that the reason?*

"Who is Cloyce?" Joey asked.

"He was a drifter who worked here for a while this summer," Jake said. "He needed food and work, and I needed a bit of help. But I'm beginning to suspect he wanted more than food."

"What do you mean?" Andy wondered.

"Easy money. If he could carry away some small tools and sell them, it would be money in his pocket."

Andy's neck began to turn red again, and Joey could see he was angry.

Jake told Andy to bring a roll of binder twine. Joey carried a posthole digger and a roll of wire, while Jake tied on a nail apron carrying staples and took a pair of pliers and a hammer.

"We'll try to tie the wires together until I get new clippers. Maybe we can cut some wire with the pliers, but that isn't easy. I hope we don't need to reset any posts. At least he left my digger behind."

"How do you know Cloyce took the clippers, Dad?

Did you see him do it?" Andy ventured to ask, struggling to hold his temper.

"No, I didn't. But who else would have taken them? I'm only suspecting he did."

After they had the fence temporarily repaired and were on the way back to the house, Andy begged, "May I please build Shep's house?"

"Not yet," answered Jake. "You and Joey can go fishing now, though, but be sure to be back in time for supper and chores. Shep's house will just have to wait."

Fishing with Joey! Andy wondered how that would turn out.

10
Old Salty

A light west wind was blowing that afternoon. Andy was glad because he often heard his dad say that's when fishing is best.

"I'd better go to town and buy some tools and fencing. We'll have to watch the cows a bit more until we get that fence fixed right. I don't think binder twine will hold them very long.

"There's not much grass left in the pasture. Throw down some hay in the barnyard so the cows have something to chew.

"Now don't you boys fish too hard!" he teased as he hitched up his horse to head for town. "You know you're worn out from the harvest."

Andy looked startled until he noticed the slight grin on his dad's face.

"Well, nau, ich weese net (well, now, I don't know)," Joey remarked. "If I get ahold of Old Salty, he's the one who'll wear out first. After I pull him out, first off, I'd

show him to my brother. We have a bet going on who will catch him."

Old Salty was the name given to that big fish down in Fish Rock Creek. Many an Amish boy tried his hand at catching him, but with a swish of his tail and a twist of his fin, he was always gone again.

"What kind of bet did you make?" Andy inquired.

"I promised him my bicycle if he hooks Old Salty and brings him to shore before I do."

"Why, Joey, how can you bet like that?" Jake Maust knew that Joey had been baptized and was a member of the church. Surely he should know that betting is a form of gambling!

"Oh, well, I was going to give him the bicycle sometime anyhow."

"And what did your brother bet?" Andy asked.

"That's a secret between him and me. Nobody else knows it," Joey answered with a dark look.

"Does your dad know about this?" Jake Maust quizzed his hired hand.

"*Mei Zeit, nee* (my time, no)!" replied Joey. "Why should we tell him? It's just a friendly bet."

"Such habits are not good and can only lead to trouble," Jake warned.

"Think about it, Joey. Provide things honest in the sight of all people. I suggest you think over that verse in Romans. Ya, even the first part of chapter 12, too. Maybe you'll change your mind. *Denk's iwwer* (think it over)."

Then Jake climbed into the buggy and left, and the boys prepared to go fishing.

Andy was mulling over Joey's words in his mind.

He was determined to find out what Johnny promised Joey if Joey won the bet.

Joey broke into his thoughts. "Come on, Andy, we need some worms if we expect to catch fish."

"I know where some big night crawlers are," Andy responded.

"Ya, where?"

"Under those old railroad ties behind the shop. The other day I moved one just a little, and there was the biggest worm I ever saw."

"Let's go dig them out. You got something to put them in?"

Andy hurried to the washhouse, where he found a tin can used to keep a bit of kerosene. Lizzie or the girls poured it from an open can when they started the fire to heat the wash water. It was safer that way.

Quickly Andy emptied its contents, grabbed an old rag, and wiped the can dry. He also went inside and got a bag of cookies. Hannah saw him but didn't try to stop him. She wanted no argument with her brother.

"What took you so long? Oh, I see. You brought something to eat. That's okay, if you share."

Andy didn't answer. He planned to eat all the cookies he wanted. After all, *his* mom had baked them—not Joey's mother.

Joey took the can that Andy handed him. "Ugh!" he exclaimed. "*Was waar drin* (what was in here)?"

"Kerosene. But I wiped it out good with a rag. The worms won't care."

"Maybe the worms won't, but the fish are not likely to go for a kerosene-coated worm."

"Okay! You go find something to put them in,"

Andy snorted, throwing the can as far as he could.

Joey could see he was riled. The back of Andy's neck began to turn red.

"There's an old trash pile in the corner of the rail fence," Joey observed. "We could surely find something there."

"You find it, then. I'll get the poles."

Each went his separate way. Joey rummaged around in the trash and returned with a battered kettle. He was glad the lid had been pitched out, too. Although it was warped, it fit well enough to keep the bait from drying out.

In a short time they dug enough night crawlers and put them in the kettle with a little moist earth. Then they were on their way.

"Does that dog have to come along?" Joey asked. He still felt uncomfortable around Shep.

"He doesn't have to, but I want him to." Andy picked up the best pole and called, "Come on, Shep. Let's go."

They fished for thirty minutes, catching a few blue gill. Then Andy hooked him! Old Salty put up a fight.

When Joey saw the struggle Andy was having, he pretended to help bring the big fish in. Andy resented this and resisted with all his might.

In the excitement, Shep thought Joey was fighting Andy. The dog made his move, knocking both boys to the ground. He stood guard over Joey.

In all the confusion, Old Salty swam away.

"*Nau guck* (now look) what you made me do. You made me drop my pole. Now Old Salty is gone. I could have brought him in, but you had to mess things up.

You wanted to make it look as if you caught him."

Even though he was now fourteen, Andy was almost in tears.

"Just get your dog away from me, and I promise I'll never bother you again at fishing or anything," Joey begged.

"I feel like making Shep pin you down all day. If you tell everyone that I really had Old Salty on the line, I'll make Shep let you go," Andy bargained.

"I will. Really, I will," Joey agreed.

That ended the fishing, but Joey was more determined than ever to keep his bet with his brother. In spite of Jake Maust's admonition, he now wished he *would* catch Old Salty. It would be worth Johnny's bet.

Indeed, it would! thought Joey as he rubbed his leg where Shep had nipped him.

11
Billy-Goat Surprise

One Sunday a year later, church services were to be held at the Lester Swartz home. Andy dreaded the teasing he often received after church dismissed.

The Amish serve a simple noon meal to those who care to stay. It is a good chance for fellowship and catching up on all the latest news.

Andy's parents generally stayed. They were well-liked and had many relatives attending.

Andy would have preferred to leave right after dismissal and spend time with the animals at home, especially if there were baby lambs, calves, chicks, or even piglets to pet and care for. He struggled with his temper, but he had a place in his heart for helpless and small things—a special tender place.

He was planning to leave for home as quickly as possible after church and a quick bite to eat at the Swartz place. It was within easy walking distance of his home, so Andy decided he could leave anytime.

Several boys his age had another idea.

"Hey, Andy," called Ezra Miller. *"Die Gees sin ausgebroche* (the goats have broken out). We need all the help we can get to herd them back to the barn. How about helping us?"

Andy was rather wary because these same boys played tricks on him at times. "No, I'm going home," he told them.

The fellows knew how to make him change his mind. "Ach, *daer ist zu fett zu schpringe* (this one is too fat to run)," mocked Noah Yutzy.

"He is afraid of *den Geesbock* (the billy goat)!" laughed Adam Chupp.

That was all it took. Andy's dander was up, and he took the challenge. "I'll show you I'm not afraid. Where are those goats?"

"Follow me," Noah said, leading the way.

Andy should have known by the smirks on their faces that they were up to no good. Instead, he thought, *You don't accuse Andy Maust of being a sissy and get away with it. I'll prove them wrong.*

Down by the creek the goats were contentedly nibbling grass. That was exactly where they were supposed to be, but Andy didn't know that.

"All right, boys, chase them over toward the creek," Ezra called out. "I'll show you a good trick."

Andy suspected something was up, but he didn't know what.

"If Billy attacks, run for the creek. I'll take care of him then," Ezra promised.

It wasn't long until the billy goat went for Noah.

"Kumm do riwwer (come over here)!" yelled Ezra.

Noah was a swift runner. He went straight for Ezra, and so did Billy.

"Schpring weck (jump aside)," shouted Ezra, giving Noah a shove. The old goat was already charging as Noah hopped out of the way. Ezra threw himself on the ground, and Billy went over him, headfirst into Fish Rock Creek.

"Es is wild (it's wild)!" exclaimed Adam.

How the boys laughed! Andy had to admit it looked funny. Yet he knew it was cruel, and he started for home.

"Wo gehst du (where are you going)?" Ezra asked.

"Home," Andy replied. "I don't think those goats broke out. You just said that."

"Aw, come on. We're just having a little fun. Why don't you try it?"

"No. It's not fun for the goat. What did he ever do to you? I'm going home."

"Buwe (boys)," Ezra declared, "Andy here is afraid of an old goat."

"Ya, you could say old Billy got his goat!" quipped Adam.

"Oh well, *der Maus ist zu fett* (the mouse is too fat). He couldn't outsmart old Billy," Noah mocked Andy to the other boys.

It was too much. Andy would show them.

Billy had come out of the water, but he was still shaking his head and stamping angrily.

"Yaagt ihn do riwwer (chase him over here)," Andy told the boys.

"Oh, no," protested Ezra. "He's angry. If we try to chase him, he'll turn on us. You get his attention, and he'll come all right." The boys stood a safe distance away and waited.

Andy began to make loud noises and waved his arms. He soon had the goat's attention. As Billy came charging, Ezra yelled, "Turn your back, Andy, and hit the ground when I tell you to."

Andy turned his back to Billy, but Ezra never told him when to drop down. Billy hit his target, and Andy flew headfirst into the water.

"Hey, Andy," Ezra groaned, "I forgot to tell you to hit the ground. How did you like the billy-goat surprise?"

Andy knew by the way the boys were laughing that Ezra hadn't forgotten. It was all planned and set up to duck him in the creek.

A strong temptation seized Andy. He wanted to run every one of those boys down and thrash them good. Even though he was sopping wet, he felt hot with anger. Why did they always pick on him?

He made his way out of the creek and headed toward home. If he had a chance to meet those boys alone, one by one, he would even the score.

"Andy," said Jake that evening, "were you down by the creek after church today?"

"Ya, Dad."

"Did you tease Lester's billy goat?"

"Sort of."

"What do you mean, 'sort of'? Either you did or you didn't."

"The other boys made me do it, Dad."

"They can't make you do anything. I want the truth, Andy. What happened?"

As Andy told the whole story, once more his anger welled up within.

"It would be best if you could ignore those fellows. Especially when they're up to mischief."

"How did you know I was at the creek?" asked Andy.

"We heard some of the boys talk about your billy-goat surprise, as they put it. And Mom saw your wet clothes on the line when we came home. Andy, if you wouldn't let it bother you so when you are teased, I believe it would stop. They pick on you because they know you'll get angry."

Jake put his hand on Andy's shoulder. "Son, we'll pray for you to gain victory over anger. It won't be easy, but it's possible."

Andy felt ashamed. He needed to be alone, so he took a few apples and went to the barn. Eating and being with nature and animals had a soothing effect on Andy.

As he listened to the contented sounds around him, Andy reflected upon the day and his dad's words. Let the boys laugh about his billy-goat surprise. Someday he would surprise them all. Wait and see!

12
Horseshoe Cave

It was a nippy Sunday afternoon. Autumn was fast drawing to a close. The Maust family had spent all day at home since it was not their church Sunday.

"Dad," Andy proposed after dinner, "I'd like to go to Horseshoe Cave before winter sets in."

"Ach, Andy, why don't you stay home and read the Bible a while? It's three miles to the cave. What do you want there?"

"Just to do something different. I might find some Indian arrowheads. Enos Byler's boys found real nice ones. Besides, I can easily walk there and back before chore time. I did read the Bible a while this morning."

"Can you remember what you read?" Lizzie quizzed him.

"Well, something about God."

"That takes in a lot, Andy," said Jake. "God is clear through the Bible. In fact, the Word is God. Look it up—John, chapter 1, verse 1."

"If we don't remember what we read, Andy, it doesn't do us much good," Lizzie told her son.

"Well, I can't read or understand the German too well, so sometimes I switch over to the English. Is that *letz* (wrong)?"

"No, it's not, but we must not forget our mother tongue. The *Deitsch* (Pennsylvania German) helps to hold us together. For generations our people have tried to preserve it and keep the plain Christian life. Some even gave their lives for it. They were burned at the stake, beheaded, thrown to the lions, and—"

"Oh, now I remember," Andy interrupted. "I read the story of Daniel in the lions' den. That's what made me think of the cave. Now may I go?" He wondered how asking for hiking permission brought on such a conversation.

"What do you say, Mom?" Jake asked his wife.

She wished that he wouldn't leave the decision to her. "Ach, *ich weese net* (I don't know). Are you sure you'll be back by chore time?"

"Ya, Mom, I will."

"Take Shep along, then," his dad advised, "and don't go too far into the cave. Be sure the flashlight has new batteries."

"Ya, Dad," Andy agreed. Yet he was thinking, *They act like I'm a child. After all, I'll be sixteen in a few months.*

Before leaving, Andy made sure he had some food to take along. He made a few sandwiches and took some meat scraps out for Shep. The dog wolfed them down, then stood looking inquiringly at his master.

"Come on, boy," Andy called. "You and I are going exploring."

The dog had no idea what exploring meant but willingly followed.

Before he reached the cave, Andy ate two sandwiches. He told himself that all this walking made him hungry again, and because he was so big, it took more to fill him.

The road he took was lightly traveled, and one Model-T was all the traffic he encountered. The driver of the car tooted his horn, and Andy waved back. Everybody was friendly in this farming area.

He did not recognize this man, but no matter. Anyone who showed kindness to him was considered a friend.

After an hour, Andy was glad to see the opening of Horseshoe Cave just ahead.

"Sure is dark in here, Shep," Andy remarked, stepping inside the entrance. "I'm not afraid, though. Lester's boys claim there are *Schpucke* (spooks) in here, but I don't believe them. Besides, Dad says there are no such things as *Schpucke*."

Slowly the boy and the dog descended farther into the cave. Sometimes Andy had to crawl to get through low openings.

"Hey, you know what, Shep? It seems to be getting lighter in here."

Andy's eyes were getting used to the change from the outside. Along the way, Shep was sniffing at any rocks or little rivulets and enjoying the adventure.

Andy spotted something shiny. He shone his flashlight on the biggest arrowhead he had ever seen.

"Look at this, Shep. Ain't it fine? Boy, wait till I show this to those Swartz boys. Ya, and to Ezra, Adam, and

Noah. *No sie sei net so schmaert* (then they won't be so smart)."

He stuffed the arrowhead into his pocket and started to go deeper into the cave. Just then Shep made a low growl.

"*Was is letz* (what's wrong)? What is it, boy?"

The dog's ears perked up. Andy knew he heard something or someone, but it was too far away to make out what it was.

There was a passageway off to Andy's left. He stepped into it and crouched behind a large boulder. Now he heard it, too. It sounded like a faint echo.

"Down, Shep," Andy whispered, pulling the dog close to him. He patted Shep gently and listened. Someone else was in the cave.

Andy and his dog waited. The voices came closer. Shep quivered, but Andy kept him under control.

Johnny Swartz, Adam Chupp, and Ezra Miller came around the corner of the main cave track. Andy glimpsed them and ducked down so they wouldn't see him. He recognized their voices.

Andy was just about ready to make his presence known when Ezra said, "Nah, *ich glaawe's net* (I don't believe it). Fat Andy Maust hooked Old Salty? Why, a lot of us boys have been trying to catch him all summer."

"My brother Joey was with him, and he claims the fat mouse would have brought him in if he hadn't interfered. I'm glad he didn't catch him, though, because Joey and I have this bet going. If I catch him, Joey has to give me his bicycle. But if he gets him. . . ."

Andy listened intently.

"Ya?" asked Ezra.

"Well," Johnny stated, "I promised to kill that Shep dog that runs with Andy. None of us like him, and we decided. . . ."

Andy had heard enough! As soon as the boys were out of earshot, he took Shep, made his way to the cave mouth, and hiked home.

It was turning colder, and Andy hurried. He went over in his mind how he would report to his dad about the Swartz boys' evil plan to kill Shep.

During chore time, Andy had his chance to tell his dad about his afternoon of exploring and eavesdropping.

"Ach," said Jake, "those boys are all talk. Johnny wouldn't do such a cruel thing."

Andy wasn't so sure!

13
Snow Boots

At last Andy turned sixteen. Jake had bought a nice horse and a used buggy for him. The buggy wasn't the best nor the horse the fastest, but Andy didn't care. Now he could leave church right after services were over. That would take care of a lot of the abuse from other boys.

He would be happy to go home and spend time with the farm animals. Andy also enjoyed being outdoors. Many people missed beauty in nature which did not escape his eyes. In fact, his sister Esther found the following poem in his pocket as she prepared to do the laundry.

GOD'S PASSING BY

Soft blows the wind
  and stirs in the treetops.
Gently the stream
  flows murmuring by.

Grass sparkles crystal
with morning's fresh dewdrops.
Be silent and listen
for God's passing by.

Yes, he saw God in nature. Some people would consider Andy a sissy for writing such things, but his family thought it was nice.

He remembered the first-place poem for which the teacher gave him the Barlow pocket knife. The title was "Winged Flight."

Although the idea for the poem had come to him several years ago, Andy remembered it well. One night a large harvest moon was riding in the sky, and the weather had turned cold. On his way from the barn to the house, he heard and saw a flock of Canada geese. It inspired Andy to write the following:

WINGED FLIGHT

Wild geese are winging, their way they are winging,
Far to the south where warm breezes blow.
A message they bring, to me they are bringing,
"Summer is over. We sense traces of snow."
"Hurry," they call, to each other, there's calling,
Honking their way through the darkening sky,
"Hurry, oh, hurry, ere snowflakes start falling,"
Shadow silhouettes 'gainst the moon as they fly.

Fly then my friends, fly in V-shape formation
Out of my sight till I see you no more.
But one, yes, the One who made all creation
Will bid you return when winter is o'er.
So I'll dream, yes, I'll dream by my warm blazing fire,

Till I see you once more skirt the silvery moon.
Then the joy of my heart will soar ever higher
And welcome you back to your summer lagoon.

Andy was not good at sports. He was always chosen last for team games. Andy was not a good runner or wrestler, but he was a good writer. No one could truthfully deny that.

He felt good when he put his thoughts down on paper. That was his private world where no one made fun of him. Many more poems were hidden away in a notebook left from his school days. The world would have been richer had he shared them.

Now it was winter again. Andy made his way to church in his own buggy for the first time. His sister Esther accompanied him.

"It's less crowded in the double buggy if I can go with you," she said.

"I don't care. But I hope you don't want to stay after church," Andy told her.

"Why not? I like to have lunch and visit with my friends. Don't you ever like staying?"

"No, I don't. How would you like it if a bunch of the girls mocked you?"

"I wouldn't. But the Wagler boys are nice to you. Why don't you just stay with them?"

"It doesn't matter who I'm with. Adam, Ezra, and Noah make fun of me. Joey and Johnny do, too. They're the worst ones."

"All right. If you want to leave right after church, I'll be ready," Esther agreed. "But you can't always run away from trouble. Dad says so."

Andy knew she was right, but he was willing to avoid it as long as he could.

As soon as Esther and Andy drove in the lane to Hostetler's, where church was being held that Sunday, it started.

"*Guck an die grosse Maus* (look at the big mouse)," announced Ezra, mocking the Maust name. "Some big guy he is now, driving his own rig."

"Hey, Maust, where did you get that fancy buggy and race horse?" Johnny Swartz called out for all to hear.

The other fellows snickered and snorted.

As Andy started to unhitch, Johnny and Noah offered, "Let us help you so your horse won't get away." Noah slapped the horse's mane lightly, and the palm of his hand stuck a clump of burrs into the horsehair.

Andy felt his temper surfacing again. He tried hard to keep it under control. Who would want to go into a church service with an angry attitude?

Then Mahlon Schrock walked over to the group, and the harassment stopped. "It's time to go inside, boys," he stated firmly.

Andy was grateful. As the boys filed into the room, Andy was seated by a window. Midway through the service, he noticed dark clouds forming and racing through the sky. Soon snow was speckling the windowpane and scudding onto the ground.

Bishop Lapp must have noticed it, too, for he began to speak of being washed whiter than snow. Andy drew his attention back to the preaching.

"Isaiah chapter 1, verse 18," the bishop repeated.

"Though your sins be as scarlet, they shall be as white as snow."

Andy thought that perhaps God could wash him clean from his temper.

By the time church let out, the snow had piled to several inches. It would be a cold ride home in his open buggy. Andy was glad they only had three miles to travel.

When he went to the closed-in porch for his *Iwwerschuh* (overshoes), they were gone. He looked everywhere he could imagine. Behind the big copper wash kettle, and even inside it.

Esther had come out for her shawl and bonnet. "What are you looking for?" she asked.

"My *Iwwerschuh,*" Andy replied. She helped her brother hunt for them.

Johnny Swartz and Ezra Miller came inside. "Looking for something?" Johnny wondered with a grin on his face.

"Ya, my *Iwwerschuh,*" Andy said. The boys just watched Esther and her brother look for the missing boots. Finally Andy approached them. "You know where they are, don't you?"

"Why don't you look outdoors if they aren't in here?" suggested Ezra.

"Ya," Johnny kidded, "maybe they got tired waiting and walked out on you."

Both boys laughed as they left the porch.

Andy remembered that these two had left the service for several minutes. Now it was plain to him. It had all been planned.

"Don't let your temper get the better of you," Esther

begged. "That's just what those boys want. I've got my boots on. I'll wade out and get yours," she offered.

"No," stated Andy, "I'll go, and this time they won't see me angry." Yet try as he could, he felt hot all over except for his feet.

"Now," he asked his sister on the way home, "do you understand why I don't like staying after church? I shook all the snow out of my boots, but my feet got wet and cold. I think I'm wearing snow boots."

Esther didn't answer. She didn't know what to say. But she did pull the heavy lap robe up around them both, and Andy knew she cared.

14
One Bad Egg

Most Amish families like singing together. The Maust family was no different.

"Why don't we invite the *Freindschaft* (relatives) over next between Sunday for a singing?" suggested Lizzie one winter evening. "We could enjoy a little more company, what with Sam and Roy and Ellie out working for others. They don't even get home on weekends much anymore."

One Sunday, church services were held in the Maust's district. The next Sunday, services were held in another district but not in theirs. This left some free Sundays for family activities, visiting, and singing.

"Ya, that would be nice," Jake agreed. "Some of the *Freindschaft* live in other districts, though, and wouldn't want to miss their services."

"Ach, *ich weese sell* (I know that)," Lizzie responded. "We'll make it for the late afternoon, and each can bring a dish or pie, cake, or whatever."

Jake saw Lizzie was getting excited about the idea.

Andy, too, enjoyed those Sunday afternoons and evenings when his extended family sang together. He had heard of *englisch* churches that had evening services, but his people did not have them.

Sometimes on Sunday his family played table games. Scrabble and Dutch Blitz were favorites. Other times they might simply share a bowl of freshly popped corn and apples along with the week's happenings.

Best of all, though, was when they gathered with hymnbooks in hand and lifted their voices in praise to God. It was a time of bonding, and at those times, Andy felt closer to his family than at any other time. He had a nice tenor voice and used it freely. Here no one made fun of him.

He was in his *Rumschpringe* stage, old enough to run around and go to youth singings. But there the same clump of boys made *Schpott* (fun) of him.

"Listen once how that Andy bellers!" exclaimed Adam Chupp.

"Ya, *er meent er kann singe* (he thinks he can sing)," snorted Johnny Swartz.

One was there who didn't make *Schpott.* Aire Mast thought Andy to be a nice-looking boy and an excellent singer. She didn't care if he was quite heavy.

Aire herself knew what it was like to struggle with keeping one's weight down. Andy was not aware of Aire's notice of him. His sister Esther and Aire were good friends, but he had decided to pay no attention to girls. Some of them had been just as unkind to him as the boys were.

Andy seldom went to young folks' singings because he couldn't sing out without being mocked. Yet many of those making fun of him were jealous of Andy's good voice. As is often the case, they put Andy down to make themselves appear better.

"Is this going to be an old folks' singing?" asked Esther. "Or can we unmarried ones come?"

"We would be glad if you younger ones joined us," Jake told her. "We need some young blood in the group. Just don't run so fast with those newer tunes that we can't catch you," he teased.

"Ach, you!" Esther wrinkled her nose at him. "I hope the Masts can come. I want Aire to see how I fixed my bedroom since Annie and Fannie left."

"Don't you miss them?" Lizzie asked.

"Sure I do, but I don't miss a crowded bedroom. It's nice to have it to myself and to have some privacy once."

"Be sure to invite Aire special, and I believe she'll come," Mother said.

Andy was glad to see the Wagler boys driving in the lane. They at least were his friends. But he was surprised when Johnny Swartz and Ezra Miller showed up. They generally didn't even help sing at young folks' gatherings. Why had they come?

Andy began to speculate. He decided three things were possible. Either they came to play some prank, to eat the good food, or try to get rid of his dog. This last thought struck terror into his heart.

Andy immediately left the house and locked Shep in the workshop. Ever since they had discovered some of Jake's tools missing, they kept the shop door locked.

Shep did not like the idea of being penned up, but Andy felt safer.

"I know, Shep," he told the dog. "As soon as those boys leave, I'll let you out."

Andy slipped back into the house, but his dad noticed him come in.

"Where have you been, Andy?" Jake asked.

"Oh, just out."

"Just out where? We were waiting for you to help set up tables."

Tables were benches set end to end and side by side. The seats were more backless benches.

Church services were to be held at Jake Maust's place in one week. The *Bankwagge* (bench wagon) had been brought to the Maust home for that event. When a family offered their house for church in two weeks, they would hitch two horses to the *Bankwagge* and bring it to their place.

Benches weren't the only thing the wagon hauled. It also contained a lost-and-found cloth bag. In it were freshly laundered hankies, diapers, baby bottles, pacifiers, and children's toys.

The toys were simple, often a string of beads or a baby rattle. Little girls had much fun peeking in to see what the bag held. Sometimes if they found a hanky that caught their eye, they kept it.

What a supper they had before the singing that evening at Jake's! Many could have sung better had they not eaten so much.

Between supper and singing, Andy's dad quizzed him again about his whereabouts before supper. When he saw his son's anger begin to rise, he decided it best to discuss it some other time. The singing went well, and Andy felt better until. . . .

The boys hadn't seen Andy in the feedway of the barn as they were preparing to leave. "*Buwe,*" remarked Ezra Miller, "did you see *Fettkessel* (lard kettle) get all red-faced and feisty when his dad asked where he was before supper?"

"Ya," answered Johnny, "and I haven't seen that old dog of his around. He probably penned him up somewhere."

"We ought to find out where and let him out," Ezra proposed.

"I wouldn't," advised Mosie Wagler. "Andy is a good boy, once you get to know him."

"Sure, only you Waglers and that Aire Mast think so. I've heard she thinks he's pretty nice, too. How nice is he when he gets so mad?"

"Well, I suppose there's one bad egg in every family," Mosie remarked.

This really hurt Andy's feelings. One of his few friends called him a bad egg. He couldn't believe it.

Andy had a hard time going to sleep that night.

15
A Good Trick

"Andy, did you lock Shep in the workshop last night?" Jake asked his son.

"Ya, Dad, I did."

"*Fer was* (why)? What did he do?"

"He didn't do anything," Andy answered.

"Then I want to know why you did it."

"I guess because I'm the bad egg of the family," Andy replied sarcastically.

"What kind of answer is that? I never heard anyone say such a thing."

"Well, I did, and from someone I *thought* was my friend."

"Are you sure? Who would ever say such a thing?"

"I'll tell you who." Andy related the previous evening's happenings. His dad listened patiently to everything.

"Let me tell you, Andy," he counseled, "sometimes it's not easy to deal with boys like Ezra and Johnny.

And I'm sure Mosie Wagler didn't mean it. He knows about your temper and your weight problem, but counts you a friend.

"Mosie did tell the boys it wasn't wise to let Shep loose. Don't put yourself down, Andy. I've heard you say that you're just a nobody. God never created a nobody.

"Think of this, Andy. God loved you enough that he sent his Son to die for you. You must be worth a great deal for him to do that."

How could Andy answer such a statement? He didn't say a word, but he did have a lot to think about.

"Now," declared Jake, "we can't lock Shep in the workshop anymore. He made a mess of things. It is a *Wunner* (wonder) he didn't get hurt. My good saw and scythe were knocked down as well as some hammers and wrenches. It's no place for a dog."

"Well, you never let me build a house for him, Dad. I kept asking for permission to make a doghouse."

"The choice was yours, Andy. Remember?"

Oh, what's the use? thought Andy. *If only I were twenty-one so I could be on my own.*

Several months later, Esther said to Andy, "I'd really like to go to singing this Sunday night. Won't you take me? Aire Mast doesn't have a way either, and I thought she could ride along."

Andy didn't go to singings very often, but Esther had just turned sixteen and wanted so much to go. His sister often did favors for him, so he could hardly refuse.

"Do we *have* to take Aire?" Andy asked.

"We don't have to, but I thought it would be neighborly. She's a nice girl and one of my best friends."

"But I don't know her very well. What will I say?"

"You probably don't need to say anything. Aire and I have no problems talking," Esther assured him.

"*Das glaawe ich* (that I believe)," laughed Andy. "Girls, they *gaxe* (cackle) like hens."

"We do not," Esther protested. "Are you taking us or aren't you?"

"Let me sleep on it," Andy teased.

"In that case, you can wait for the half-moon pies until you've slept. I made some fresh this morning."

"Tell you what. If you give me some of those pies, I'll promise right now to take you."

Esther knew Andy's weak spot. It must be true, she thought, that the way to a man's heart is through his stomach.

Andy ate two half-moon pies, and Esther got her promise.

"You won't change your mind, will you?" she asked her brother.

"Well, now that the half-moon pies are gone, I just might," Andy said mischievously.

"Oh, no, the pies aren't gone. There are plenty more where those came from."

"In that case, then, I'll be sure to keep my promise."

Sunday arrived, and as their custom was, the family went to church. Esther could hardly wait to tell Aire that they would take her along to the singing. It had all been arranged.

"We'll pick you up around seven."

"I'll be ready," Aire said.

True to Esther's statement, Andy need not have

worried about making conversation. The girls kept up a lively session all the way to the singing.

The buggy was built to seat two comfortably. Since Aire was more on the stout side she sat beside Andy and held Esther, who was a sprite of a girl.

When they arrived at the Mullet home where the singing was being held, Andy stopped by the front gate. As the girls stepped from the buggy, Andy told Esther, "Let's not stay too long."

His sister just smiled and nodded. She wondered what he considered *too* long.

"Your brother doesn't care much for singing, does he?" Aire remarked as Andy went to tie his horse to the hitching post.

"Oh, he loves to sing. It's just that some young folks give him a hard time."

"I've noticed," said Aire. "I think it's cruel and un-Christian."

"Yes, it is, but I wish he wouldn't let it bother him so. Dad says if he wouldn't let it upset him, the boys would quit."

"That sounds like my parents. Oh, Esther, I know something about Andy's pain. The Swartz girls and some others say pretty mean things about me. It isn't easy."

"Oh, Aire!" exclaimed Esther in surprise. "I didn't know."

"Es macht nix aus (it doesn't matter)," Aire stated. "Come on, let's go inside."

But it did matter. It mattered to Esther, for Aire was a nice girl and her friend.

To Andy's relief, none of his tormentors were present and singing went well. He freely sang from his heart. His clear tenor voice carried across the room and blended well with others.

He forgot about time and couldn't believe it when the parting hymn was announced. The song which always ended the singing was "Blest Be the Tie That Binds." Then everyone was joking and visiting for a while.

Before Andy went to get his rig, Esther pulled him aside for a private word. "I have something to tell you. Don't be upset with me, but one of the boys just asked to take me home.

"I talked to Aire about it, and she said she doesn't mind driving home with you. Andy, I've waited so long for him to ask me. I hope you're not angry, because I told him I'd go along."

Andy was speechless. Did his sister have this in mind all along? What could he do since his Esther had promised? He guessed the fellow was Louis Farmwald, but Esther was trying to keep it a secret. So Andy just shrugged in agreement, and soon Esther was out the door into the dark to catch a ride—her first date.

This had been the most enjoyable evening Andy had ever spent with the *Yunge* (young folks). He would try not to spoil it now. But he certainly wished the ride home were over with.

"This is very nice of you, Andy," Aire remarked as she got into the buggy. "Maybe I could have gone home with the Rabers, but they would need to drive out of the way. Since you go right by my place, I hope you don't mind."

"Ya," Andy replied, "I go right by."

They drove through the spring night, with only the sound of the horse's hooves and the buggy wheels crunching on the gravel road. *Why can't I think of something to say?* Andy wondered. He was not comfortable with this strained silence between them.

For want of anything better to talk about, Andy blurted out, "*Wie viel Kieh melkst du* (how many cows do you milk)?" As soon as the words left his mouth, he felt foolish. What a thing to say!

Aire, however, promptly answered, "Altogether we milk fifteen. I myself milk four. Do you like animals, Andy? I do."

Her response to his silly question was so natural, and without making fun of him, that Andy felt at ease and risked talking some more.

"Oh, I sure do like animals. They seem to understand me better than some people do. Ach, I bet you think I talk *dumm* (dumb)," he said rather lamely.

"Not at all," Aire assured him. "Believe me, Andy, I know what it's like not to be accepted by some of the *Yunge*. Mom says not to let it bother me, but it's easier said than done."

Here was someone experiencing what Andy was all too familiar with. The ice between them was broken, and for the first time in his life, Andy paid attention to a girl. The talk flowed better now as they shared and built up a layer of trust in each other.

As they neared the Mast home, Aire spoke further of her feelings. "Andy, I've really enjoyed this evening, especially the ride home. Your sister seemed to play a trick on us, but I'd say it was a good trick." She laughed with a light trill.

Andy liked the sound of that laugh. It seemed musical, not harsh and mocking as he heard so often from the boys. She had said his name several times, and that felt good.

Andy did not consider her bold or forward. No, she was genuine and friendly. He liked that.

As she turned toward the house, Andy said, "Good night. Maybe Esther can play a trick like this on us again sometime."

"Maybe!" And again Aire laughed with that delightful trill.

Andy started his horse toward home. What a wonderful evening this had been! He would never forget it. As he drove along in the friendly dark, he sang the parting hymn again:

The fellowship of kindred minds
  Is like to that above.

16
The Big News

It was splashed all over the front page of the town's weekly paper. The headline read "Local Youth Catches Big Fish!"

The account started with a flourish: "Joey Swartz, son of Lester Swartz, hooked the Big One in Fish Rock Creek. Old Salty (as he was known to all) finally met his match. The bass measured twenty-three and a half inches and weighed in at eight pounds, the biggest fish ever caught in this neck of the woods.

"Joey said he has sold the fish to Ben Howland, owner of the hardware store under the town clock. Howland plans to have a taxidermist mount Old Salty and put him on display in the store above the fishing tackle. Under the Big One will be a bronze plaque with the date of the catch and Joey Swartz's name."

On another page an article gave the details of how Joey Swartz landed Old Salty. It told of the mighty fight the fish put up, and it explained Joey's strategy in bringing him in. Still another article was on what the mighty fisherman used—kind of bait, type of equipment, weight of line, and on and on.

A picture of the big bass was displayed on the front page. Next to the picture was a statement that said Mr. Swartz declined having his picture taken as it is *verbodde* (forbidden) by the Amish, and Joey was a member of that church.

"I wonder," Andy quipped, after reading the glowing account, "whether it would be more sinful for Joey to have his picture taken or to have the pride he carries."

"Andy, be careful what you say. Are you sure you're not jealous?" his dad probed him.

"Sure, I wanted to catch Old Salty, but for a different reason."

"Don't tell me you still think the Swartz boys will carry out that silly bet they made?"

That is exactly what Andy thought. Evidently his dad didn't know those boys. Perhaps he was giving them the benefit of the doubt, as he often advised Andy to do. But why can't he ever believe me? Andy mused.

The Sunday following the big news, that was all the youth talked about before and after church services. Joey Swartz's chest was puffed out, and he strutted importantly.

Joey even pushed his hat to an angle, rakishly to one side, which also was forbidden by the church. But this was Joey's day, and he would bask in the attention while he could.

Andy was sick of all the fuss. Only one thing lifted

his spirits. His sister Esther wanted to take Aire Mast along to the singing with them again that evening.

Andy soberly agreed and tried to hide his delight. Esther would likely have another ride home—with Louis? He suspected that they were seeing each other regularly now. That meant that Aire and Andy would be by themselves on the trip back from the singing.

Shep was happy to see Andy come home from church. He followed his master all during evening chores. During the week the dog had run behind the mower in the fields. He liked to chase after rabbits and other wildlife flushed out as the hay was cut. By evening he was one tired dog.

But church Sunday was different. Everyone was gone, and it was lonesome. He lay on the new hay and slept most of the day away. Now he jumped around Andy's legs, frisky and wanting to play.

"Come on, Shep," Andy protested. "I'm in a hurry to get these chores done. I'll play fetch with you another time." He reached down and patted the soft furry coat.

That evening Aire was ready when Andy and Esther pulled up to her gate.

"Are we late?" Andy asked.

"No, I just came to sit on the porch swing when I saw your buggy turn the corner."

Andy let Esther and Aire carry on the talking until they arrived at the farm home that was hosting the young people's gathering.

Joey and his buddies were at the singing but did not even come inside. They thought it more fun to rehash the account of catching Old Salty. Each time Joey told the story, the exploit grew more glorious.

With Ezra, Joey, Johnny, and Noah out back, Andy again sang unhindered. The only unpleasant encounter with them was upon leaving.

As Andy stopped at the yard gate to pick up Aire, in the darkness, Johnny called out, "*Die Fettkessel* (lard kettle) express is leaving."

Uproarious laughter followed them out the farm lane.

"*Ich dauere selli Buwe* (I feel sorry for those boys)," said Aire.

"They'll bring *Druwwel* (trouble) upon themselves." Andy tried to sound wise.

As they turned onto the road, Andy decided to change the subject. "Sure is a nice evening. Dad says he thinks we're in for a hot summer."

"Ya, our garden is coming along well. Of course, Mom believes in planting according to the zodiac signs. Does *your* mother do that?" Aire asked.

"She plants everything by the moon or signs. I don't pay much attention, though. Dad says he plants in the ground, not in signs." They laughed together at that remark.

"Mom is real strict about planting potatoes in full moon and cucumbers in the sign of the fish," Aire added.

"Speaking of fish," Andy put in, "did you read the write-ups about Joey Swartz and his catch?"

"I did, and even if I hadn't, I sure heard about it after church today," Aire answered.

"What do you think about it?" Andy asked. "I just hope Joey doesn't let this go to his head. He walked around pretty *grossfeilich* (stuck-up) today."

"Ya, I noticed that, too. His sister was bragging and telling around that he had a bet going with someone that he'd catch that fish."

Aire could not understand why Andy gasped as though shocked. He tensed up, and she wondered if she had said something out of order.

"What is it? Did I say something wrong?"

"No," Andy assured her, "you didn't say anything wrong. It's just that I can't understand that Joey."

He did not tell her that he knew what the bet was. Andy wanted this evening to be an enjoyable one, and he would not spoil it by telling Aire of his fears.

As soon as he got home, Andy looked for Shep. The dog bounded from the barn to meet him. After unhitching and putting his horse in her stall, Andy talked firmly to Shep.

"You stay in the barn, you hear? Don't wander off our place to chase after rabbits or anything. Shep, I hope you understand."

Andy latched the barn door securely and went to the house. There he spent a restless night.

What would happen now? Would Johnny really carry out his bet?

17

Who's to Blame?

Two months passed, threshing was over, and the excitement concerning the big fish story had quieted down. Andy was beginning to feel more hopeful.

Perhaps Johnny Swartz would not keep his bet. Or perhaps Joey, as a baptized member of the church, would release his brother from his promise to kill Shep.

"Take the *Wagge* (wagon) into town, Andy, and get the horses shod. Bring some chicken feed and treated posts along home," directed Jake. "I'd go myself, but I have to work on my tax papers.

"We need four corner posts by the east pasture. Something has been working on the wood, and they're rotting out. I suspect it's termites, so I want well-treated posts."

Andy liked taking the sorrel team. Shep ran around in circles as his master got the team and wagon ready. He followed Andy out the drive and down the road.

When Andy discovered that Shep was trailing along, he ordered him to go home. Shep kept on following. It wasn't like him to disobey.

Andy stopped the team and spit out harsh words: "Git! Git on home!"

The dog hesitated a bit.

"Go on, Shep!" Andy shouted as he pretended to throw something at him. This was totally out of character for his master. The dog turned back and slunk toward home with his head hanging down and his tail between his legs.

Andy felt badly about his tone of voice and his dog's reaction. Yet he knew it was for Shep's own good. When I get home, I'll make it up to him, Andy decided.

But when he got home, no Shep came running to meet him. He must be hiding in the barn, sulking because of the way I sent him home, Andy thought.

He called Shep, but his dog did not come. He began to look for him, continuing to call, but still no dog appeared. Andy became alarmed.

"Dad," he asked, "have you seen Shep? I can't find him."

"I haven't seen him since this morning when you were getting ready to leave. He ran around like he was full of all the pep and vigor in the world."

"He followed me down the road a ways. I had to tell him several times to go home. I'm afraid I spoke too roughly to him.

"The last I saw, he turned and walked slowly toward our place. Do you think he's hiding from me? Or worse yet, maybe he ran away."

"No, my guess is he flushed a quail or rabbit and

took off into the woods," suggested Jake with a chuckle. "You know how he likes to explore. I think he'll be snooping around Fish Rock and the woods. Give him time; he'll come home."

But Shep didn't come home, not that day nor the next, nor even the next. By this time, Jake suspected something was amiss. He went with Andy along the creek bank and through the woods, hunting and calling. All was in vain.

"I just know that Johnny Swartz made good his bet," Andy agonized. "I'm of a mind to go over there and beat up on him. *Ich kann ihn nemme* (I can take him)," he boasted angrily.

"You'll do no such thing, Andy," Jake declared. "To begin with, we have no proof that Johnny had anything to do with Shep's disappearance."

"Well, what do you expect? Do you think Johnny will come, bringing Shep to our front door, saying, 'Here he is. I killed him'?"

"Of course not," Jake replied. "But we don't know where Shep is."

"I've got a pretty good idea," Andy muttered. He was angrier than he'd ever been.

For the first time in Andy's life, he didn't care to eat. His appetite had left him. It had now been a week since Shep was gone.

Andy was supposed to disc the field bordering the creek to get it ready for planting winter wheat. He had worked several hours when he noticed a pair of vultures circling just above the trash pile. As his team came closer, the vultures drifted higher in the air, waiting.

Andy was determined to see what the fuss was about, so he stopped his team to take a look. But he was not ready for what he saw. There lay his beloved dog Shep, with evidence of a clean shot through his head.

Andy couldn't bear to look. He turned away with tears blinding his eyes and said, "Oh, Shep, I didn't mean it. I didn't mean to scold you. Why did this have to happen?"

He stumbled back to the disc and his patient team. Somehow he kept working until the sun was high overhead and it was lunchtime. Lunch—who can eat? he wondered bitterly.

"Dad, I found Shep," Andy said.

"I told you we'd find him. Where is he?"

"He is down at the edge of the rail fence, shot clean through the head, thrown on the trash pile like so much junk."

"No," gasped Lizzie.

Esther was shocked, too, and so was Fannie, who was home for the fall harvest season.

"Ya, and I know who did it," Andy told them. "It was Johnny Swartz."

"I've told you before, Andy, we can't blame people unless we have proof. We'll go bury Shep right after lunch, and then tonight I'll go and have a talk with Lester Swartz and his boys."

"That won't do any good, Dad. Those boys have told the untruth before. Do you really think they'll admit it if they are to blame?"

"I don't know if they are or not. All we can do is our own part."

Andy didn't want any lunch. He dreaded seeing Shep again, but he would rather bury him than leave him to the vultures.

A plan was forming in Andy's mind. If the Swartz boys got away with this, and if his dad still gave them the benefit of the doubt, Andy knew what he would do.

He wasn't going to tell anyone, not his mother or sisters. No, not even Aire. She wouldn't want to see him anymore if she knew of his plan. It might be best that way.

18
What About Andy?

The house was quiet except for sounds floating through the open window, the chirping of tree frogs, and an occasional hoot from a screech owl. Andy lay in bed thinking of the events of the last several weeks.

The Swartz boys emphatically denied killing his dog. He knew they would. It seemed to Andy that his Dad believed Joey and Johnny.

"Well then," said Andy softly to himself, "let Joey or Johnny work for Dad. I'm going to see the world. No need staying around here where I'm not appreciated. I'm going to be a drifter like Cloyce was and see me some sights."

Andy knew it was a bad time of the year to leave. There was wheat to be planted, second-cutting hay to bring in, and corn to cut in a few weeks. But he would not let that stop him. A roving man is what he would be.

The words of a song Cloyce Rader sang drifted back

to him. "Give me land, lots of land under starry skies above. Don't fence me in." That was all he remembered. His mind was made up. He'd leave this very night.

Andy tried to remember what Cloyce carried. He removed a pillowcase from one of his pillows. Then he thought about the guitar, and wished he had a musical instrument to take along. Somehow he would learn to play it like Cloyce did.

Quietly Andy pulled open a dresser drawer. He took two clean shirts and put them into the empty pillowcase. Socks and underwear were added to the list. He threw in a comb and a toothbrush, then stuffed in a spare pair of trousers to complete what he thought was sufficient.

His eyes momentarily looked at the Bible on his bedside stand. It had been a gift from his parents on his twelfth birthday. Should he take it? For a second Andy hesitated. Then he reached out, took it, and put it deep inside his makeshift bag. Just in case I want something to read, Andy reasoned.

Now he had one more decision to make. Should he leave a note? Andy really did love his parents, although like other Amish, he didn't say much about it. After all, actions speak louder than words.

There was no paper or pencil in Andy's bedroom. He didn't want to chance taking some from the living room desk. He noticed his flashlight, which he surely didn't want to leave behind.

Stepping softly in his sock feet, flashlight in one hand and belongings in the other, he made his way downstairs. On the way out he grabbed his jacket from the hook by the back door. Then he sat on the edge of the porch to put on his shoes.

As he reached the gate, there lay a piece of paper. Andy saw it plainly by moonlight. It was a receipt from the grain elevator in town. He took it to the shop, placed it backside up on the workbench, and in the glow of the flashlight, he scribbled hurriedly.

Mom and Dad—

Don't worry.
I'll be all right.
Just had to get away.
Andy

He returned to the house and quickly and quietly placed the note inside the kitchen screen door. Without so much as a backward glance, he was gone.

"*Was is das* (what is this)?" Lizzie said, picking up a piece of paper from the kitchen floor. She was getting ready to prepare breakfast when she saw it. Jake had opened the stairway door and was calling Andy to get up to help with the chores.

"I don't see why that boy doesn't answer. Looks like it'll be a nice day, and we should get in the field early. Andy, come on!" he called again.

"Ach, Jake, look at this." Lizzie handed him the note that Andy left for them.

"Nah!" Jake exclaimed. "It can't be." He made his way upstairs to Andy's room. It was empty.

The girls heard that something was amiss. Esther and Fannie came out of their room. Ordinarily Dad never came upstairs.

"What is it, Dad?" they asked. "Is someone sick?"

"It's Andy," Jake moaned in a voice barely audible. "He's gone."

"Gone?" gasped Esther. "Gone where?"

"I don't know. He left during the night."

The girls and Lizzie had to go to Andy's bedroom to see for themselves. They just couldn't believe it.

"I'll help chore this morning," Esther said.

"If Mom can spare me, I'll help in the field in Andy's place," Fannie offered.

"First thing," Jake remarked, "I'm going over to Lester's, and I'll see if his boys know anything about this.

"This will be hard on Grandpa and Grandma. They thought a lot of Andy. Maybe if he hadn't been teased so much. . . . Perhaps it seemed to Andy as if I took the word of others instead of believing him."

"We must not blame ourselves," Lizzie said, wiping tears. "We did what we thought best."

No one was hungry at breakfast. Work had to be done, and so each one mechanically helped.

The Lester Swartz family was shocked at the news.

"Ever since Andy found his dog shot through the head, he was not the same," Jake told Lester and his boys. "He refused to eat and I was worried. That boy was always a big eater. Lately he was moody and losing weight.

"Now he's gone, and I don't know what to make of it. Are you boys sure you don't know anything about this? You had nothing to do with killing Shep? Did Andy make any threats about running away?"

"No, we didn't have anything to do with putting

Shep out of the way," Johnny Swartz answered. "But I must say I had promised Joey here I would if he caught Old Salty. I'm ashamed to admit that I made such a bet.

"But I did not do it, and I don't know who did. I never heard Andy say anything about leaving. Did you, Joey?"

"Nope," answered Joey. "I didn't. Maybe he left because we called him names. Now I wish we hadn't."

Both boys felt ill at ease and avoided looking at their neighbor.

"We will hope and pray. Perhaps he'll change his mind and come back soon," Jake said.

"Ya, *mir hoffe* (we hope)," Lester agreed.

• • •

But what about Andy? Where was he going? He had taken no food, and his family guessed that he had only two or three dollars in his pocket.

His parents and siblings wondered how he was getting along.

"I only hope our prayers will follow him," Lizzie told her family.

19
Life of a Rover

The sun was not far above the horizon when Andy woke up. He felt as if he had walked for many miles.

Away in the distance, he heard a train whistle for a crossing. He wondered if that could be the six-thirty freight. Checking his pocket watch, he saw it was indeed six-thirty.

Andy had walked until three in the morning. He found a soft patch of mossy grass in Grover's Woods and laid down to rest a bit.

He pulled his jacket tightly around him and used some brush and leaves for cover. Finally he fell asleep, worn out from working all day and hiking at night.

Now he was startled by the sunrise. Dew clung to his hair and clothes, and he shivered.

Andy talked to himself: "I'll warm up soon enough, once I start walking. Wouldn't it be something now if I met Cloyce while I'm rambling around!

"Until I'm further from home, I'll stick to back roads

and woods. People in this area might recognize me. By tonight I might be near Breck's Crossing, and if I'm lucky I can catch a train there."

Cloyce had told Andy how he had hopped a freight several times. Andy thought it sounded so exciting. He remembered the very words as though hearing them again this morning.

"Yes sir, boy," Cloyce had told him. "That's some adventure. You hear the whistle blow a long way off. It's best to hop a freight at night. When you hear that lonesome whistle, make your run for the crossing. Stay out of sight until she stops to take on water."

Andy wondered why Cloyce always referred to a train as "she." He hadn't questioned him about it.

"Watch the billy as he checks the boxcars. If you see a car carryin' hay or straw, grab it. Don't take an empty one—no place to hide. Steer clear of the billy."

The billy was the man riding the caboose. He made his rounds when the train stopped and checked for drifters stealing a ride. He carried a big stick called a billy club, and that's how he got his name.

In midmorning Andy was passing an apple orchard. Apples were ripe and smelled sweet in the sunshine. There was no house in sight.

For the first time, Andy felt hungry. For the first time, he did something he had never done before. Reaching across the fence, he took that which did not belong to him.

He slipped half a dozen apples into his makeshift knapsack and began to eat one as he walked. Yet even as he did so, he remembered words of wisdom passed down in his family and drilled into him at home:

Kind, lass allein
was nicht ist dein.
(Child, leave alone
what you don't own).

For a moment Andy felt a sharp pang of guilt. But only for a moment. The sweet juicy taste of the early harvest won out, and soon he ate two more. *After all,* he thought, *didn't Jesus' disciples pluck and eat ears of corn as they walked through a field?*

He was thirsty. Well, he would keep walking. Andy reasoned that he would find water somehow, perhaps when he crossed a stream.

His shoe rubbed a blister on his heel. Nighttime couldn't come soon enough. At least then he could give his feet a rest.

Andy left the woods and the dirt trail he had been following as he reached a dusty gravel road. The house he saw in the distance didn't look familiar. He began talking to himself again.

"I wonder now if it would be safe to stop and ask for a bite to eat, like Cloyce did at our place. At least maybe I could get a drink of water." His mouth was dry, and the apples didn't quite satisfy him.

"I'm going to chance it. Nothing ventured, nothing gained. The least they can do is say no."

A barking dog came to meet this stranger. He wagged his tail all the while, so Andy knew he must be friendly. "Hello, old boy," he said, patting him.

In answer to Andy's knock, a plump lady gingerly opened the door and looked him over. "Yes, what do you want?"

"I was wondering if you could give me a little something to eat and a drink of water?"

"Well, I don't have much," she claimed, in hope of discouraging Andy. She had never seen an Amish boy before and was skeptical. He was dressed in a quaint style and had such a strange haircut. It was shaped like a round bowl.

"Ach," said Andy, "I don't need much. A piece of bread and butter will do. And a drink of water," he added as though it were an afterthought.

Why, he even talks funny, thought the woman. *I wonder where he's from. Maybe he broke out of an institution. But I suppose the quickest way to be rid of him is to feed him.*

"If you sit out under the large maple, I'll fix you something," she promised warily.

"Could I have a glass of water first?" Andy asked. "My *Hals*—I mean, my throat is so dry."

Now she was alarmed, but she decided it was best to cooperate.

"I'll get it and set it on the porch for you. Just sit under the tree. You can come and get it after I put it out."

It dawned on Andy that she didn't trust him. That unsettled him, until he remembered how his mother felt about drifters.

The lady opened the door wide enough to set a tall glass of water out for Andy. She quickly closed it again.

Pausing only a second, Andy walked over to get the water, tipped it up, and drank it all down. It was so cool and refreshing. Then he waited.

As he was ready to give up any hope for food, the door opened once more and the woman set a plate of food out on the edge of the porch.

"Here, Boomer," she called to her dog.

"Watch," she commanded, as though Boomer were a fierce guard dog.

Obediently the dog went to the side of his mistress. But Andy laughed to himself. It struck him as funny that Boomer would scare anyone. Not with that tail wagging!

"Leave the plate and glass on the porch," the woman said as she retreated into the house.

"*Danki*—er, thank you,"Andy stammered as the door closed. He wanted to ask for more water, but kept quiet because he didn't want to make her uneasy any more than necessary.

Andy was used to giving thanks at each meal, so he bowed his head in silent prayer before he ate.

He felt odd, though. Would God hear him since he was running away? Had he done so wrong? But surely God knew how he was hurting. His dog was dead. Others made fun of him. And did his dad care?

The plate of food contained an egg sandwich and, of all things, an apple. Andy ate the sandwich gratefully but put the apple with the others.

He set the empty glass and plate on the porch and left. As he turned onto the road, he saw the curtain flutter at the window, so he knew he was being watched.

So this is the life of a rover! he thought. *Well, tonight I'll try to hop a freight. There has to be a town I'll reach before long, a place where trains stop.*

Things will be better tonight, Andy assured himself.

20
Hopping a Freight

It took another day and a half of walking before Andy came to a town. The first thing he noticed was the railroad crossing and the water tower. To him, this was a welcome sight.

Along the way, Andy narrowly escaped an angry bull who charged him as he cut through a pasture field. A dog took a piece from his one pant leg, and once as he sat on a stump to rest, a bunch of yellow jackets attacked.

He was ready for some of the good life Cloyce had told him about. His three dollars wouldn't last very long, and he had eaten about all the apples he could handle. He knew he needed to find food to be ready for what lay ahead.

Tonight he would try to ride the train as far as it would go. Maybe then he could find work for several weeks, at least.

Andy made his way into the small town and found a

little diner. The sign in the window said,

Hamburgers	15 cents
French Fries	10 cents
Large Root Beer	5 cents

Andy didn't know what French fries were, but he decided to find out. Stepping inside, Andy was greeted by the delicious smell of food and a swarthy-faced proprietor. The place was empty except for a surly-looking man back in the corner.

"Howdy," the owner addressed Andy. "What can I get you?"

"Hi," Andy responded. "I'd like a hamburger, some fries, and a glass of water."

"How you want that hamburg done?"

"Cooked."

"You tryin' to be sassy?"

"No," said Andy. He didn't know what this fellow meant. Andy had never been in a restaurant before, and he was used to eating things as they came.

"Well, how do you want it: well, medium, or rare?"

Figuring he might as well get his money's worth, Andy replied, "All three."

Taking Andy by the shirt collar, the man shook him and barked, "I'm not askin' again. Either you tell me how you want it, or I'll get Lefty here to throw you out in the street."

"Well—," Andy blurted out.

"That's more like it. Now sit down and stay put until I get your food ready."

The irate cook didn't know that Andy was going to

say, "Well, that's all right. I've changed my mind." He didn't let Andy get past the word *well*.

The fellow called Lefty got up and sat next to Andy. "Where you from?" he asked.

"Rosemont." Andy wished Lefty had stayed in the corner where he was.

"Never heard of the place. I knew you weren't from around here. How come you wear them silly-looking clothes?"

"These are all I have." Andy didn't want to continue the conversation.

"Yeah? Well, where you goin'?"

Andy hated to face so many questions. "I'd like to go to Kansas or Iowa," he answered.

"Boy, that's a fur piece. How you 'spect t'git there?"

"I'd like to go by train."

"Oh, hoppin' the freight!" Lefty laughed like it was a joke. "Hey, Pop," he called to the owner. "Hey, Pop, this one wants to take the freight to Iowa or Kansas. Some greenhorn. Don't even know these trains run north or south."

Pop chuckled as he brought the greasy food and set it on the small counter.

Andy started to bow his head, then changed his mind and began to eat hurriedly. He wanted to get away from this place. As different as the food was, Andy ate with relish. He paid his bill and prepared to leave.

"Hey, Greenhorn," Lefty blared out. "If you play your cards right, you could make the 9:45 to Alabama. I hear tell they're takin' on a lot of cotton pickers. Might earn you enough fer other clothes." He roared with that rowdy laugh again.

Andy gave him a little wave but didn't answer as he left. Lefty had given him information he was seeking. At last he knew what time the freight would come through and where it was going.

Andy waited on the edge of town behind a ramshackle building with a sign that read FIX-IT SHOP. He felt better since his supper. The bee stings were still uncomfortable, however.

He wished for a bath or even just a place to wash his face and hands and brush his teeth. Well, soon he planned to be in Alabama picking cotton. Once he made some money, he could buy things he needed.

Darkness began to settle over the land. Most everything was quiet after a few noisy children were called in from their play. A dog barked, a door slammed, and the town seemed to go to sleep.

"But I must not go to sleep," Andy told himself. "No siree. I have to catch that 9:45 freight."

He pulled out his pocket watch and for the umteenth time checked it. Only ten after eight. Andy stretched out on the grass and dozed off.

Then in the distance he heard the lonesome whistle. Picking up his pack and stretching his legs, he waited. Now he could hear the rumble as the engine light came into view. Andy stayed in the shadows and crept closer. Black smoke belched from the stack as the train groaned to a stop.

"Open 'er up, Jake," the engineer called to the brakey as they dismounted. They got ready to take on water. The billy began to check each car and shone his flashlight under the car and behind the wheels, too.

"All right, get out of there," he said, as he slid the door of a boxcar wide open. "Come on, move along. This is no passenger car."

He flourished his billy club as he threatened a seedy-looking character who climbed stiffly from the train. "Don't let me catch you again," he warned as he marched the culprit down the track away from the train.

Andy saw his chance. The door to the boxcar was still open. He ran and climbed aboard. There was some straw in this car, but it smelled of cattle. Andy didn't care, though. He was just glad to be inside something that would travel faster than walking.

Soon he heard footsteps approaching. Andy hardly breathed as he scrunched far into the corner behind straw he had piled up. To his relief the door of the car slammed shut, and he heard the latch hammered home on the outside. He settled down with a sigh.

After a while the train began to groan and rumble as it started on its way.

"Alabama bound!" someone said.

Andy jumped. He thought he was all alone. Quickly he rummaged for his flashlight and shone its beam around the boxcar. There was the roughest-looking fellow he had ever seen in his life!

"Scared you, didn't I?" said the man in a gruff voice.

Andy didn't answer. He was shaking all over. The man flashed an evil grin.

"I ain't gonna hurt you, boy. Just make sure you don't get in my way. When this train stops, I get off first. You hear?"

Andy only nodded.

"We'll get into Junction Alabama about daybreak. I know. I rode this line before. As we slow down, I'm gonna force the door open before the billy gets here. I've done it many times. Then I'll jump just before the train stops.

"Remember, keep out of my way!"

Andy wouldn't forget. He certainly wanted no trouble from this character.

21

Put Your Back to It!

The next afternoon as the train slowed, the intruder lost no time in forcing the latch with an iron bar and sliding the door open. He left in a hurry, and with him went Andy's belongings. This stranger grabbed the pillowcase and all it held.

"Likely expecting to find money in my backpack," Andy mumbled.

He had no time to waste. Looking out the half-open door, he saw the billy coming. The billy spotted Andy as soon as he jumped.

"Hey, you there," he yelled at him. "Don't you ever let me see you around here again. How did you get out of that car, anyway? I'll have you—"

Andy didn't hear the rest as he was almost out of earshot and running hard.

Beyond the depot he saw a wooded area. That is where he went, staying behind houses, bushes, and whatever offered protection. In the woods, Andy discovered a small flowing stream. The water looked cool and inviting, so he stooped and drank.

Here he was, lapping water like an animal. This wasn't at all like Cloyce made drifting out to be. Things would get better. He was sure of it.

Andy rested for a while. He lay back and enjoyed the song of birds. It bothered him, though, that his belongings were gone.

He thought he might pray and ask God to help him. Somehow that didn't seem right. He was running from troubles at home, but now he realized that he had brought more trouble upon himself. Was it fair to expect God to give him an easy way out?

Andy knew he could find work and buy some clothes and other necessities. But the Bible his parents had given him could not be replaced. Oh, he could buy another one, but it wouldn't mean as much to him.

He remembered what his mom had written on the inside of the front cover:

> Sin will keep you from this Book,
> or this Book will keep you from sin.

Andy got up and ambled into town. His legs felt stiff, and his clothes were getting loose on him. He was glad for his suspenders, but even so his pants looked baggy.

He saw a small wooden sign crudely lettered JUNCTION. This must be the town mentioned by the rover in the boxcar. Andy was walking down the wooden sidewalk when he spotted a sign in the window of a saloon:

PICKERS WANTED
INQUIRE WITHIN

Andy hesitated. He had never been in a saloon before, but he was desperate. All he wanted was a job.

Several unkempt men lounged at the counter. They looked up as Andy entered.

"You want something?" asked a large man coming from a side room.

"Ya, I saw your sign. I need work," Andy told him.

"Hey, Rafe," yelled the man, turning to the room he just came from.

At the doorway, the dirty faded curtain parted. Out stepped a short man with an ugly scar on his cheek. Andy thought he looked mean.

"Yeah, what you want?"

"This Baggy Britches wants work."

Was Andy being dubbed with a nickname again? At home it was *Fettkessel* (lard kettle). Now this!

"So!" Rafe eyed Andy. He walked slowly around him and sized him up for a farm boy. Rafe asked, "Ever pick cotton?"

"No, but I'm willing to learn."

They talked a while longer, then Rafe said sternly, "I'll try you, boy, but you'd better put your back to it. Get some pants that fit, or you'll be trippin' all over yourself."

"I can't. My things were all stolen on my way here."

"We will fix you up with something. Can't have those baggy britches hamperin' you. Where you stayin'?"

"I just got here, and I'll be looking for a place."

"Jud," Rafe called the big man whom Andy first met. "Take Baggy Britches here down to the shanties and give him a bunk and some clothes that he can work in. Get him started pickin' first thing in the morning. Mind now," he addressed Andy, "you put your back to it."

How often Andy was to hear those words the next few months. He felt worldly, wearing *englisch* (non-Amish) clothes. They were not made like the Amish clothes he was used to.

He felt sinful, sleeping in the dirty shack and eating strange food at the same table with his cursing co-workers. His hair needed cutting, and they gave him a different haircut. He felt so *englisch*.

Andy knew what he would do first thing, once he got paid. Many times he thought of home. He wondered who was helping on the farm in his place.

How did Mother take it when he left? Were Esther and Fannie worried about him? Did Grandpa and Grandma Maust think he was bad? And what about Aire? What had she said?

Two weeks before picking was over, the men were given half of their pay. It was not very much because Rafe deducted most of it for lodging, food, and the clothes he supplied for Andy.

He told the men in no uncertain terms that the rest of the wages would be paid once the fields were clean. Andy took his pay and went straight to the bank and the post office.

Andy needed some postcards. He was ready to let his parents know where he was. A week before, he had stopped at a small church and listened to folks inside singing. He heard the words "Child, come home, Child, come home." It touched his heart. At least he would write.

As Andy waited his turn to have his check cashed, he noticed a poster on the wall to his left. He looked the second time. No, it couldn't be true. But there it was—a picture of Cloyce.

Above the picture was one word: "WANTED." Beneath the picture appeared the words

FOR MURDER

Reward: Five thousand dollars

Clyde Reber,
alias Charles Cater,
alias Chuck Gebert,
alias Cloyce Rader

Andy was shocked. At the post office, he saw the same picture and notice. It was hard to believe. To think that his family had sheltered a criminal!

He had intended to try to get to Kansas or Iowa. Now he felt sick of the idea. Cloyce had painted the drifter's life as pleasant and good. But for him, it was only a way to hide from the law.

Andy was done with it. A sudden homesickness swept over him. He would give up Kansas, Iowa, and any other plans.

Most of his fellow workers were taking their money for an evening in the saloon. "Come on, Andy," a few tried to encourage him. "Live a little. Take some of your money and come to the bar and pool hall with us.

You never do anything for fun. Just work, work, work!"

Andy suspected that they just wanted to get their hands on some of his money. He had wisely deposited most of his pay in the bank to save for further travel. Now it would pay his train fare home. This time he would have a ticket and need not fear being put off the train.

He bought as plain a pair of pants and shirt as possible, but they weren't Amish made. How would it be accepted by his family and community? Bending his back to the task of picking cotton had taken its toll. He ate little and was much thinner than when he left.

Would he be a foreigner when he returned? Andy missed the farm and the animals. Somehow his loss of Shep didn't seem so important anymore. Oh, he would still miss his dog, but it didn't seem worthwhile arguing about who killed him.

Andy sent the card off that very evening.

Dear Family—

I'm okay.
I'm coming home.
Andy

That was all he wrote.

22
The Prodigal Returns!

No words could bring more joy to the Maust family than the few on that card.

"Mom!" squealed Esther. "I brought the mail in, and there's a card from Andy."

"*Wunderbaar* (wonderful)!" Lizzie cried out, clutching her throat. "Where is he? What did he write?" she asked breathlessly.

"I don't know where he is," Esther answered, "but he's coming home."

"Oh, *danke Gott* (thank God)!" Lizzie exclaimed. "Let me see that card," she demanded, reaching for it.

She sat down on a chair and read it. Turning it over and over, savoring every word, she remarked, "Why, it's from Alabama. Ach, my! How in the *Welt* (world) did he get way down there?

"I wish Dad were here so he could read this. It will make him so happy. We can't keep it from him till suppertime. Esther, you take this to the end of the cornfield. I think he and Johnny are cutting corn by hand to open the field for the binder."

"Ya, Mom, I'll go right away."

Esther was happy to be the bearer of such good news. Even though it had been about six weeks since Andy had left, it seemed much longer.

Jake was busy tying a bundle of cornstalks and didn't see his daughter approaching, but Johnny did. Johnny Swartz had helped Jake since Andy left.

"Here comes Esther," Johnny said.

"*Was is letz* (what's wrong)?" Jake asked. Alarm showed in his voice.

"*Nix, nix is letz* (nothing, nothing's wrong)," Esther assured him. "Here, read this." She handed the card to her father.

Jake read the postcard and cleared his throat. He took his big blue work handkerchief from his pocket and blew his nose. Trying to hide his emotions, he forced a cough.

Esther and Johnny saw a tear escape the corner of his eye and roll down his cheek. He quickly brushed it away as if he were shooing a fly.

Finally Jake said in an unnatural voice, "I'm glad." He gave the card back to Esther.

"What did Mom have to say?" he asked.

"She said, 'Thank God.' Did you see that the card is mailed from a town in Alabama? Mom wondered how he got there. She wanted you to hear the good news as soon as we could let you know. Ya, Mom cried, but I think it's because she's happy."

"I know it is," Jake agreed.

"Well, I'm relieved, too, that he is coming home,"

Johnny put in. "We boys were pretty hard on him sometimes. That will change now. I hope since we found out what happened to your dog, uh, I mean his dog, that Andy will forgive us. Do you think Andy will believe us when you tell him about Shep?"

"Yes, Johnny, I think he will."

The Amish are close-knit families, and since the Mausts knew many of the relatives and friends were concerned, they shared the glad news. It only took a day for everyone in the community to hear that Andy was coming home.

Both sets of grandparents wept and rejoiced with the Maust family. But none was happier than Aire Mast. She hoped their friendship would take up where they had been when Andy left.

"Esther," she asked the next Sunday, "do you think Andy has forgotten me?"

"Of course not, Aire. He wouldn't forget you."

Andy had not written when he would be home, only that he was coming. Day after day the family watched. At evening they wondered if he might come during the night.

"Waiting for Andy is like watching and praying for Someone else to come. Only that waiting is even more important because we are to be ready then to go with him. Are we watching and praying as eagerly for Christ to come as we are for Andy?" Jake asked his household. It was a soul-searching thought.

Andy had only one more week of work for Rafe. That seemed like the longest week of his life. He was so glad to get out of that smoke-filled shanty and away from those foul-mouthed men.

He felt his parents and others must be praying for him. That thought helped him to make it through and head for home.

His train ticket was in his pocket, and the rest of his pay was safely put into traveler's checks. The banker advised Andy to do this when he heard that Andy was riding the train.

"Can't be too careful nowadays, you know," he warned. "Hard telling what kind of riffraff ride that line. Why, I've heard of some people who lost all their luggage and money. Mind you, they lost everything they carried!"

Andy remembered how he had been robbed on the train coming south, but he didn't discuss it. Besides, he was going honestly by passenger car this time.

With mixed emotions Andy settled comfortably in a seat by himself. The train was not full, and Andy was glad. He wanted to be alone.

His mind was drawn to a story in the Bible. He had read it many times in Luke, chapter 15. Yes, he thought, I'm that prodigal son. Let's hope my father is as ready to take me back as that father was in the story.

There was no train through his hometown. Andy didn't mind. Once before he had walked the distance. This time he need not keep to the back roads or woods.

Andy had not gone far after leaving the train station until he caught a ride with a local farmer in his truck. He dropped off Andy a half mile from his home.

How good the fields of ripened corn looked, and the rustling of its dry leaves was music to his ears. He took in all the familiar sights.

Slowly he made his way to the house. Lizzie heard

the door open and looked up into the face of her youngest son. Breakfast was just about ready and, oh, it smelled so good to Andy.

"Andy!" exclaimed Lizzie. "Is that you?"

"Ya, Mom."

She gave him a tight hug.

Jake came from the washroom where he was cleaning up from morning chores.

"Hello, Dad," Andy said hesitantly, not knowing how he would be received.

"Welcome home, Andy!" Jake exclaimed as he gave him a bear hug. "Sit down. Breakfast is soon ready. We always set a plate for you in case. . . ."

Jake had to stop. His eyes were watery, and he swallowed hard before he said, "You're so thin. Didn't you get enough to eat?"

"I had food, but it wasn't as good as what I smell now."

"You're *englisch!*" Lizzie remarked.

"Only because my other clothes were stolen or didn't fit anymore."

"We'll make others, the girls and I, won't we?" she said, looking at Esther and Fannie, who stood speechless at the change in their brother's appearance.

"Ya," they agreed.

Johnny came over to help Jake with the day's work.

Jake met him at the door. "Thanks for your help this fall, Johnny, but I don't need you anymore. Andy's home!"

"Oh, that's good! Now let me tell him about Shep," Johnny begged.

"Andy, I'm glad you're home," Johnny said warmly

as he stepped into the farm kitchen. "We didn't kill Shep, but we found out who did. It was two *englisch* hunters. They told us they didn't know whose dog it was. One of them was aiming for a rabbit, and just as he pulled the trigger, Shep chased the rabbit and got hit. I'm sorry."

"I believe you. I'm sorry I ever blamed you."

"But you had reason to."

"Let's call it forgotten," Andy said.

After Johnny left, Andy told them all about Cloyce. They too were shocked.

"That's what made this prodigal decide to come home. I saw how I had been misled," Andy admitted.

"Well," whispered Esther, "I know someone who will be very happy to hear the prodigal is back."

"Who?" Andy asked.

Esther mouthed words to him with no sounds: "Aire Mast."

Andy blushed.

Home—oh, it was the nicest place on earth!

23
No Greener Grass

The week after Andy returned home was so different from Alabama— cold and blustery. Yet he was glad because it was a perfect excuse not to go to singing that first Sunday evening.

"Come on, Andy," Esther begged him. "You've been home all day. People are asking about you. You'll be surprised to see so many new faces among us *Yunge* (young folks)!"

"No, I don't think I'll go this time. It's so chilly and rainy. I'm surprised you're going."

"Ach, she won't mind the weather as long as somebody picks her up at the end of the lane," Lizzie teased.

"But somebody isn't coming to take me to singing tonight. He went to Illinois with his folks for a funeral," Esther said.

"Is it a relative of the family?"

"Yes, his nephew. The child was only two years old."

"What happened?" asked Andy.

"The little boy slipped through the gate into the outside yard and was run over by the milk truck."

"*Ach, du liebe* (oh, my goodness)!" exclaimed Lizzie. "I must send a card, even if I don't know the family. Can you get their address for me, Esther?"

"Oh, I'm sure I can," her daughter said.

How like our people, thought Andy. They are so kind and sharing. Not at all like Cloyce Rader or the hard foreman in the cotton fields.

In his heart he knew there were good-hearted persons elsewhere. But it just made him happy to be part of his own people again, people he could trust.

"Sure you won't change your mind about taking me tonight?" Esther coaxed.

"Don't believe I will. I'll stay inside by this warm fire."

Andy also realized that he didn't want to be seen among the other young folks until he looked Amish again. His hair had not yet grown long enough to be cut in the Amish style.

And his dark-blue serge Sunday suit hung loose on him when he tried it for size. Lizzie had quickly made everyday clothes for him, but she had never made a man's Sunday suit.

"I'll order a new suit from Bertha Kauffman," Lizzie promised her son. "*Sie dut gute Arewet* (she does good work)."

Bertha was a single woman who worked as a *Maut* (hired girl) in other Amish homes and sewed men's Sunday suits.

"I hope she doesn't have a lot of orders lined up

right now," Lizzie mused.

"So do I," Andy agreed. "I'd like to have mine done before long."

"*Well, was welle mir duh* (well, what do we want to do)?" Esther wondered.

"Since you don't want to go to singing, Andy, what do you suggest we do as a family?" asked Jake.

"Oh, I don't know. Guess I'm content to listen to the rest of you talk, and I'll spend my time eating popcorn."

Sunday evening after chores was always popcorn time. Everyone looked forward to relaxing and spending a peaceful evening together.

"I know what we could talk about," proposed Fannie. "Andy, tell us about the green grass where you were and what you did there?"

"What do you mean by green grass?" Andy asked, astonished.

"Well," answered his sister, "Johnny Swartz said you thought the grass was greener on the other side of the fence, so you went away."

Jake, Lizzie, and Esther wished Fannie hadn't said that, but Andy only smiled.

"Johnny was right, you know," Andy finally remarked. "I guess that's exactly what I thought."

"Will you?" begged Esther.

"Will I what?" Andy said.

"Tell us what happened to you while you were gone."

"Now don't pester him if he'd rather not talk about it," Jake cautioned his daughters.

"Maybe it would be good if I'd get it out in the

open," Andy offered. "I'm ashamed of what I did and truly sorry, but you have a right to know what happened. Give me a few minutes to think how to say things."

Lizzie told them she would get the evening snack ready, but first she made her way to the bedroom and her dresser drawer for a large handkerchief. Somehow she knew she would need one.

"I'll pop the corn, Esther," she said. "You go to the basement and bring a bowl of apples. Fannie, get the dishes ready for popcorn and bring a plate of cookies from the pantry."

"Do we have any sweet cider left?" Jake asked.

"Yes, there are two full jugs in the cellarway," Lizzie told him.

Jake started to get up to get a jug to enjoy with the rest of their snack.

"I'll get it," volunteered Andy.

Soon they were seated in the farm kitchen, warmed by the cookstove. Rain was pelting against the dark window. As Andy looked at the circle of contented faces lit by the lamplight, he wondered how he could ever have left home.

Esther broke in on his musings as she blurted out, "*Fang mol aa* (start once)!"

"It isn't going to be easy," said Andy slowly. "But then, I suppose it's never easy to talk about our wrongs. I had to take so many teasings, I just thought I couldn't take any more.

"Then when I found Shep and knew someone had killed him, I let my temper get the best of me again. All I could think of was the stories Cloyce Rader told. The world he described seemed so wonderful.

"When I left, I walked the woods and back lanes until I got beyond our people. It was chilly at night. Once I stopped at a place for food, and the lady seemed afraid of me. Miles and miles I walked. My feet were blistered, and I found out what real hunger was.

"Then I reached the train station. I wanted to go to Kansas and follow the harvest, as I've heard other boys have done. But it was too late in the season, and anyhow that train was headed for Alabama.

"First I stopped for something to eat. I wasn't treated too nice, and most fellows I met were rough. I hopped on a boxcar because I didn't have enough money for a ticket. Before I got off, another bum stole everything I had except what I was wearing."

At this, Lizzie blew her nose and dried her free-flowing tears.

Andy told of working in the hot cotton fields and of his harsh treatment there. He explained that at first he lost weight while traveling because he didn't have enough food. Then he lost some more because of the long, hard hours of picking cotton.

He admitted that he just didn't feel like eating much because of the strain of adjusting to strange surroundings and southern food.

"Enough!" Lizzie didn't care to hear more. "You're home now. That's what counts most. And you won't go hungry here." She handed him a cookie.

"What made you decide to come home?" Jake asked.

"Well, I got my first pay and went to the bank. There I saw a picture of Cloyce, and he was wanted by the law. Right then and there, I knew I didn't want a life like that."

"*Ich bin froh* (I'm glad)!" Lizzie said, blowing her nose again.

"Andy," Jake told his son, "you went away a boy, and you came back a man. I'm glad you remembered who you are and didn't turn rough like those other fellows."

"What about the grass?" asked Esther. "Was it really greener?"

"No," answered Andy, "it certainly wasn't. There is none greener than in my own front yard."

His family was welcoming him home, and that was all that mattered.

24
The Road Back

Several weeks had passed since Andy came home. Other than going over to see Bertha Kauffman for a fitting of his new suit, Andy had stayed around home.

"I'll cut your hair tonight," Lizzie informed her son. "It's grown out enough now."

"Well, I'm ready," Andy remarked.

"Does that mean you'll be ready to go to *die Gmee* (church)?" Esther asked.

"Well, I don't know if Bertha will have my new suit ready yet," Andy answered.

"You know well enough she didn't have anyone else to sew for during the last three weeks. Andy, I think you're stalling. You don't want to go to church or singing, do you?" Esther challenged him.

This put Andy on the spot! However, he answered truthfully. "To be honest," he said, *"Ich shemm mich* (I'm ashamed)."

Jake heard what his son said and tried to assure him.

"Andy, you need not be ashamed of mending your ways. The shame would be if you would have remained out in worldly living. It will be a long road back, perhaps, but with God's help you can make it. We must put our past behind us and strive *zu duh besser* (to do better). Now let's get that hair cut."

Fannie and Esther were glad that Andy looked like their brother again.

"Give me two more weeks," begged Andy, "and then if Bertha has my suit ready, I'll go to church."

"And to singing?" Esther asked.

"Maybe," he answered.

"What are you afraid of? Is it Aire? You think you might run into her?"

That was exactly what Andy dreaded. He wanted to see Aire again, and yet he didn't want to. What could he say to her? Would she understand? Would she believe he was ashamed and sorry for what he had done?

Aire seemed like such a nice person. Andy doubted she ever did wrong. Well, if he gave in to Esther and went to singing, he would sit far back in the room. Perhaps if he sat behind taller boys, she wouldn't notice him.

The first snow was coming down in squalls on Monday morning a week later. Jake started laying out his plans for the day.

"Andy, I want you to take Star and go over to Lef Sam's and see if I can borrow his wedge. We need to split more wood, and a lot of those pieces are too big for the axe alone."

"I'll go right after breakfast, Dad," Andy replied.

Star pulled the buggy along at a brisk pace. Andy

whistled happily. Then he saw it. Something or someone was in the road in front of him. As he drew nearer, he could see a girl standing in the road, holding her horse. When he pulled alongside, he could tell that a shaft of her buggy was broken.

"Was is letz (what's wrong)?" Andy asked.

How astonished he was as Aire Mast looked up from her dilemma and said, "Hello, Andy."

"Oh, uh . . . hi, Aire."

"My horse shied away from Erkle's vegetable truck and acted up so badly that the one shaft broke."

"You can hardly drive with only one shaft," Andy observed.

"No, not really," laughed Aire. Once more Andy noticed the musical lilt to her laugh.

"Let me unhitch your horse and tie her behind my buggy," Andy suggested. "Then I'll take you home to get help."

"Oh, would you? I didn't know what to do. It's getting pretty cold."

"I'd be glad to," Andy said. "Here, you get in my rig and *deck dich zu* (cover yourself) with my lap robe."

Andy tied Aire's horse securely behind his buggy. Aire couldn't help but notice how gentle Andy was in handling her horse. Then he rolled her buggy off to the side of the road.

"Now," said Andy, "let's turn this outfit around, and I'll soon have you home. You had better stay inside. That wind is whipping up pretty good."

Aire liked all this attention, especially from Andy. She wanted to ask him where he had been, but restrained herself. Instead she said, "I'm sure glad you're home, Andy, and that you came by just now."

"So am I," Andy agreed.

"Oh, but where were you going?" Aire asked.

"Over to Lef Sam's to borrow a wood-splitting wedge," he answered.

"Ach, you're driving out of your way to take me home."

"Don't worry. I don't mind," Andy assured her.

"*Was is los* (what's the matter)?" Aire's dad asked as Andy drove up to the front gate. Joe Mast had just come from the house and saw them driving in the lane.

"Betsy shied and acted up at Erkle's truck and broke a buggy shaft," Aire told her father.

"Where is the rig now?" Joe inquired.

"Off the edge of the road, about a mile east on forty-two," Andy replied.

"*Danki fer die Aire heem hole* (thanks for bringing Aire home)," Joe said.

"Ya," Andy replied.

Joe untied Betsy and led her toward the barn.

Aire wished Andy didn't need to leave. There were so many things she wanted to talk about.

"I missed you at the singings," she confided as she stepped down from the buggy. "Are you coming this Sunday?"

"Maybe . . . ," Andy answered. Then as an afterthought, he asked, "Are you?"

"I'd like to if I have a way." The minute she said it, she felt as if she were hinting.

However, it was a good opportunity for Andy, and he took it. "Would you go with me?" he asked almost shyly.

"If you really want me to. I hope you didn't ask just because I said I'd go if I had a way," Aire remarked, blushing prettily.

"I really want you to go with me," Andy assured her.

"Well, good!" said Aire.

"Then meet me at the end of your lane at seven o'clock on Sunday evening," Andy instructed her.

"Fine, I'll see you then," Aire responded as she turned toward the house.

They both knew it was usual for Amish young people to keep their courtship secret and to keep their families guessing.

This was only a beginning of many Sunday evenings they would spend together.

Andy was late getting home from his errand at Lef Sam's.

"What took you so long?" Jake asked as Andy got out of the buggy.

"I took Aire Mast home. Her horse acted up for her and broke a buggy shaft."

Esther laughed when she heard about it. "A likely story!"

"Es is waahr (it is true)," Andy defended himself.

Esther believed it, but she had to tease her brother a bit. It was so much like before he ran away. She was delighted when Andy left early for the Sunday evening singing. He had only made comments about giving his horse some exercise—but Esther knew better.

The next day she told Andy, "You are on the 'road back' just as though you'd never left. I'm glad."

Four months after Andy began keeping company

with Aire, he asked her to go with no one else but him.

Most of the *Yunge* (young folks) accepted Andy and no longer made fun of him. Now if only Aire would consent to be his *Aldi* (girlfriend), the road back would seem smooth enough.

25
The Answer

Time passed quickly, and Andy and Aire were becoming best friends.

"I never thought I could be as comfortable in the company of a girl," Andy told Aire late one Saturday night at her place. The rest of her family was in bed. "When we are together, I feel right at home."

"*Sell macht mich froh* (that makes me glad)." Aire's laugh trilled again in a way that thrilled Andy.

"Remember the first time I took dinner at your house?" Andy asked. "I was so nervous I poured gravy into my coffee instead of *Raahm* (cream)."

"Well, I can see how that could happen," Aire comforted him. "The cream and gravy pitchers looked alike."

"How I wished no one would have caught what happened," Andy admitted. "I knew you did, though, because you insisted on replacing my coffee right away."

"*Du meenst net* (you don't mean)!" Aire exclaimed.

"Don't mean what?" Andy asked.

"Why, you don't mean you would have drunk that coffee anyway!"

"That's for sure what I planned to do," Andy assured her.

"*Ach, helf die aarme* (oh, help the poor)!" Aire exclaimed.

Recalling that incident was a bonding experience for them. Now Andy became silent. Aire detected a serious expression stealing across his face.

"What is it, Andy?" she asked. "Why are you so quiet?"

The couple was sitting on a swing glider under the grape arbor at Aire's home.

"I was thinking how things have changed since I came home. Aire, have you thought of baptism and joining our church?"

Aire was surprised. "Why, Andy, I just talked to Mom this very week about being *gedaaft* (baptized)."

"Did you really? Oh, it seems things are falling in place. Do you think God has a special plan for us?"

"What do you mean, Andy?" she asked.

Andy hadn't quite planned it this way, and he began to stutter. "I . . . I thought . . . you and me—maybe we could—oh, maybe we could start instruction for baptism at the same time and after that. . . ." Andy's voice trailed off, and he didn't finish his sentence.

"Ya," Aire prodded, "and after that—what were you going to say?"

"After that, . . . maybe we could get married."

There, he had said it.

"Don't you think you should ask me first?" teased Aire.

"Well, would you?" Andy asked.

His face felt so warm, and the palms of his hands were sweaty. Why was he so nervous again? They had just talked of how at home they felt in each other's company. It seemed to Andy that Aire was still very much at ease. *Why am I not more relaxed?* he wondered.

Aire paused a moment, and then she said, "I must have some time, Andy, to pray and think about this. Baptism and marriage are two very important steps in our lives. Don't you think so?"

"Oh, yes, they are," Andy agreed.

He wondered how long he would have to wait for his answer concerning marriage. Was Aire doubtful about spending the rest of her life with a former runaway? Perhaps she couldn't trust him.

Andy imagined that she thought, *When the going gets rough, he might leave me—he left his own family.*

Maybe he had no right to ask her. Yet, why would she keep company with him at all if she didn't care for him?

"You're so quiet again, Andy. Is it something I said?"

"It's just that I have no right to expect that you'd want a former drifter for a husband. *Vergess das ich dich gfrogt hab* (forget I asked you)," Andy moaned, placing his head in his hands.

"Why, Andy!" Aire cried. "I didn't think any such thing! Every girl needs time to ponder before giving an answer to such an important decision.

"Don't you ever think I'd let your past make a difference! That shall never come between us. You're sorry for what you did, and I've seen such a change in your life."

"You have?" Andy mumbled.

"Andy, I think a great deal of you. There's no one else I would even consider for a husband. I just want to be sure I'm ready and that I'd be good enough for you," Aire declared.

"Good enough!" Andy exclaimed. "Good enough? If anything, you'd be far too good for me."

"Let's get a drink of water," Aire said. "And I think there are some cookes left in the pantry."

Andy followed her, wondering all the while when she would give an answer.

Fall came early, and with it the last gathering of garden produce and crops.

"Raymond Troyers are having a corn-husking bee next Wednesday night," Andy told Aire. "Want to go?"

"That sounds like fun. Let's go."

Later Aire found out that Esther and Louis were going, too. "Why not make it a foursome? I'll ask Esther if we can use the surrey and go together."

Esther agreed it would make for a good time, and so that's what they did. The two couples sang hymns most of the way to the frolic. There was a full moon, just right for corn husking.

After the work was done in the field, everyone was invited to the house for sweet cider and apples.

"What was all the screaming about just before you *Yunge* left the field?" Raymond asked.

"A poor little mouse ran across Savilla Yutzy's shoe," Joey Swartz said.

"Well, I suppose that yelling scared the mouse more than it scared the girls," laughed Raymond.

That mouse reminded Andy of how the boys used to mock his Maust name and call him a *Maus* (mouse). Tonight they could have called that mouse his relative, but they didn't, and Andy felt accepted by all the *Yunge*. Now he felt more sure of himself, that he might even have laughed off such a joke.

On their way home, Louis said, "Do you folks know that instruction class will begin next Sunday for those desiring baptism?"

Aire glanced at Andy from the corner of her eye. She knew *she* intended to be one of the applicants. She wondered about Andy.

"Ya, I'm planning to join," Andy said.

Aire was thrilled.

"What about you, Louis?" Andy asked.

"No, I think I'll wait until spring. I want to go to Florida for several weeks this winter. If I begin instruction now, I would miss too many sessions."

"I'm going to wait and take instruction at the same time Louis does," Esther added. "Aire, are you taking instruction now?"

"Yes, I am," she answered.

"Well nau, gebt's Hochzich (well now, is there a wedding in the plans)?" teased Louis.

Esther and Louis laughed over this question.

Quickly Andy answered, "I haven't heard anything about it."

Now Aire began to think more about Andy's patience in waiting for a reply to his proposal. She spoke to her parents and treasured their advice.

"Times are hard," they said, "but if you and Andy work together and always put the Lord first in your marriage, it'll work."

Two weeks later on their way home from singing, Andy finally heard those words he longed to hear.

"Andy, if you still want to get married, I'll marry you."

"When?" was all he could think to say.

"Maybe two weeks after we become members of the church. Would that suit you?"

Would it ever! He would be ready now!

"It would suit me fine. Can you get everything ready by then? Weddings are a lot of work, you know."

"Oh, I've been getting my quilts made, putting up canned goods, and doing my sewing, just in case." Aire added that lilting laugh that Andy liked so much.

"Why, you knew all along!" Andy remarked. But he didn't mind the suspense she had kept him in.

What was it his dad had said? "You went away a boy, and you came back a man."

Now he felt like a man—a man walking tall, for at last he had his answer!

The Author

Mary Christner Borntrager was born at Plain City, Ohio, seventh in a family of ten. She was raised in the Amish faith, and according to custom, her schooling was considered complete with eight grades. In later years, Mary attended teacher-training institute at Eastern Mennonite College, Harrisonburg, Virginia. She taught at a Christian day school for seven years.

At age nineteen Mary married John Borntrager. After their four children were grown, Mary earned a certificate in childcare and youth social work from the University of Wisconsin. For twelve years, she and her late husband worked with neglected and emotionally disturbed youth.

Mary loves to write poetry and novels. She is a member of the Ohioana Library Association. A local television station and many other groups have invited her to tell about Ellie's People, her series of books, *Ellie, Rebecca, Rachel, Daniel, Reuben,* and *Andy*. A young writers' convention gave her an opportunity to speak to 150 junior-high students and review their compositions.

Involvement with the extended church family means much to Mary. She is an active member of the Hartville Mennonite congregation, a substitute Sunday school teacher, and has carried various responsibilities there. Her hobbies include Bible memory, quilting, embroidery work, table games, and reading good books. She lives at North Canton, Ohio, and keeps in touch with her eleven grandchildren and two great-grandchildren.

Mary is grateful for the many opportunities to share her faith and joy in living. Her desire is that her series, Ellie's People, will bring joy to readers, clarify misconceptions about the Amish, and break social barriers.